APPEARANCE OF MAGIC

Quantum Talents Series

TIME FOR PSYQ

Also by David M W Powers (with colleagues)

Machine Learning of Natural Language
Autonomy and Unmanned Vehicles
Teaching Skills with Virtual Humans

Also by Marti Ward

Casindra Lost
Casindra Prey (forthcoming)
Moraturi Lost
Moraturi Ring
Moraturi Star (forthcoming)
School for PsyQ (forthcoming)

With thanks to Kain Massin, Rob Bleckly and the Blackwood Writers Group for their support and encouragement, feedback and suggestions.

Quantum Talents Series

TIME FOR PSYQ

Marti Ward

Time for PsyQ
Kindle paperback edition ISBN-13: 9798385581344
Kindle hardback edition ISBN-13: 9798397447775

First published by SupRes: 2023
10 9 8 7 6 5 4 3 2 1

Front cover art: David M W Powers
Set in 12.5pt Cambria

TABLE OF CONTENTS

BONUS SCIENCE FOR PSYQ BY AIRLIE (LINK)

HEROINE'S FOREWORD

by Airlie

I am really embarrassed by this. But Marti Ward says that if this intro bit were just called Foreword or Preface, nobody would read it. But then, when I pushed him on this, he admitted that that was a bit of hyperbole, that is he is exaggerating. What he really means is almost nobody would read it, or hardly anybody would read it.

Actually, my name isn't really Airlie Sanderson, and Marti isn't really Marti Ward. My pseudonym and my friends' aliases are to protect the innocent. It's not my place to tell you why Marti uses one, but I will tell you that we went even further to protect the guilty: we don't even give them names, just designations. We don't even give away their nationality. Nor mine for that matter.

But that's not what I want to talk about. It is the science that I need to apologize about: to those who don't like science, because there is too much detail; and to those who do like science, because there is too little detail. As Aesop said, you can't please everyone and, if you try to, you won't please anyone — I hope you know his fable about the man, the boy and the donkey.

So in short, we're going to please ourselves and write the story we would like to read, and that my PsyQ friends need to read.

7

If you don't like science, you can skim what my friends call nerdy theories and explanations. Actually most of them seem to turn half their brains off when I spout like that (the *left* half). And hey, nobody says I'm always *right* — and they're still my friends.

If you do like science, or are interested in learning about the world we live in and how things work, you could stop each time I talk science and look in Wikipedia or google it, or you can click over any time to my essay on <u>Brain</u> or <u>Quantum</u> *Science for PsyQ*. Basically you can treat that like a glossary, so you can also look up things as you go, or like a bibliography to look up further info when you've finished *Time for PsyQ*: there are pointers to a mix of popular science articles and websites, as well as some important papers from the research literature.

When I wrote the first version of *Science for PsyQ* as a school project (by popular demand of the PsyQ students and their parents and teachers, not to mention the Minor Crimes police officers), I included lots of pictures. Unfortunately for various reasons I can't include them all here (size and cost and copyright and how colour pictures come out in black-and-white printed books).

Oh! By the way, this book is written in International English not American or British English, and uses the metric system. So that's why you see things like 'colour' and 'metres' rather than 'color' and 'yards' — just don't read too much into it. Remember, we are not allowed to give away the country these events occurred in. Anyway, the language of science is metric.

Airlie (and *Kate* and *Libby* and *Marti*), https://martiward.blogspot.com
Bordertown (just visiting one of many places with some such name)
August 2023

PART ONE

HOME

Chapter 1

As the first edge of sun appeared over the horizon, Airlie leapt out of bed and grabbed her clothes. The sun was still only a thin slither as she raced down the stairs. She could hear Mum in the kitchen, but it was her 11th birthday and her eyes fixated on a box wrapped in birthday paper and tied with a pink ribbon.

The box had holes punched in the top.

Airlie picked it up gently, the weight shifting awkwardly with a scrabble of claws. A sudden flash startled her, followed by "Gotcha!" and a plaintive meow.

Airlie managed to set the box down again without too much of a bump, and the box went quiet for a moment before the meowing resumed in earnest. She glared at her brother who smirked right back at her, saying. "You know you're not allowed to open your presents till we are all at the table."

But soon they were all seated, except for an excited Airlie with a meowing box on her chair. Dad smiled and said, "Happy Birthday, Airlie! I think you'll need to open that one first. It's from all of us!"

Airlie hadn't even managed to get the lid off before two black paws appeared, and then two golden orbs alongside a charcoal nose.

They looked at each other for a long moment, before Airlie reached out to pick up the kitten and cuddled it to her chest, stroking the silky fur and burying her nose into the nutmeggy scent.

"What's her name?"

"*His* name is up to you," Mum answered.

"Up-to-you is a funny name," quipped Peter, but Airlie ignored him.

"His name is Sooty!"

Sooty looked up for a moment as if to consider the name, and seemed to nod approvingly before burrowing back into Airlie's arms.

Even though Airlie's other presents were great, including the new Brain Computer Interface kit she'd asked for, somehow Sooty seemed to take all the attention.

Looking after a kitten was more work than Airlie had expected, but just as much fun. Sooty would hide in all sorts of places and keep track of who went where.

Everyone but Dad said "I thought I saw a Sooty cat" every time they spotted him... but mostly they didn't. Though quickly Airlie learnt to pretend not to notice him, because if he thought he hadn't been seen he'd leap out as she went past. Then he'd race on ahead till she went past again, follow for a while, then race ahead and hide again.

That's when Dad would say "Airlie had a little cat whose fur was black as soot", and Airlie would respond "And everywhere that I go his sooty foot he puts." Dad always complained that she didn't get that right, that the rhyme and rhythm were wrong, but Airlie had learned about this at school and said that she was a first person not a third person, and present thank you very much.

But in reality, Airlie always knew where Sooty was, and Sooty knew she knew… and the other way round too. He also seemed to know exactly where she was heading, and would make sure he got there first — suitably hidden of course.

Sooty's favourite spot was the window ledge in the sun. Of course, exactly which window that was depended on the time of day. Airlie thought that he'd like school too, but Dad said the *Mary had a little lamb* song proved there was a rule against that, although Airlie checked and there wasn't one in the official school rules.

So Sooty waited on the front window ledge, leaping off and racing to the door to greet her after school; and Airlie gave Sooty private lessons once they'd had something to eat and adjourned to her room (as Dad liked to put it).

Then came the day of the theft.

Airlie and her friends, Yan and Lilly had just got back to homeroom when she found that her pencil case was missing: the one with the shiny black cat stickers on it. Then Lilly squealed, saying her ruler was missing. Almost everyone had something missing, and Mr Rodgers said that just because someone hadn't noticed anything missing didn't mean they were the thief. He made everyone take everything out of their bags and put in on the desk so that he could see they didn't have anything with someone else's name on it.

Airlie had so much in her bag that she wasn't sure it would all fit on her desk, and some of it she hadn't even remembered being there, and of course she had no idea if anything else was missing.

After a certain amount of borrowing of pens and pencils and things, Mr Rodgers eventually managed to shift his very upset class into what ended up being a rather short maths lesson, but he promised that he would follow up on the thefts with the principal.

Airlie couldn't help sobbing as she told Mum and Dad about it after school, even though Mum said not to worry, it was only a few dollars, and they could get a new one at the shops tomorrow, and some more cat stickers and coloured pencils and everything. But Airlie insisted it wouldn't be the same, commenting in a serious voice, "It's not the dollar value but the centy mental value that's important."

Sooty tried to take her mind off it too. After all, she had a real black kitten. Wasn't that better than black cat stickers?

Sooty listened very carefully to Airlie, and made encouraging noises as she thought back through her day. Somehow having Sooty on her lap and caressing her seemed to sharpen her memories.

After eating their lunch, she and Lilly and Yan had been skipping rope in the playground, and one time when it was her turn, she remembered a boy coming from the direction of her classroom. As they concentrated, the recollection seemed to sharpen and from the corner of her eye, Airlie could actually see him slip out of the classroom and pull the door to, as he caught her attention. She didn't know his name, but thought he was a year six student.

But what to do? Should she say something to somebody?

Peter was in year six: perhaps he knew the kid?

As if in response to her question, she heard Peter arrive home from cricket practice. She raced down and perched on her chair as Mum brought him his afternoon tea.

"Did you hear about the thefts today?" Airlie asked.

"Today, no... But on Monday most of our class was missing something, but I didn't seem to have lost anything. Although today I couldn't find my lucky cricket ball. Why? Do you know something about it?"

"Maybe... We had thefts from our bags at lunchtime today, and almost all of us were missing something."

"Wow! That's just like what happened to us on Monday. Did you lose anything?"

"My pencil case with the cat stickers was stolen, but Mum's taking me to the shops tomorrow to replace everything... I think I may have seen who did it..."

"Who?"

"A boy in your year... I don't know his name, but he has light brown hair and is a bit chunky."

"Oh! That sounds like it might be Chunky," Peter suggested. "It's almost too perfect that you use that word to describe him though."

"Yes indeed," Mum said from the kitchen doorway. "You can't just make accusations. You should tell your teachers exactly what you saw, and if you can really recognize the boy — you Airlie, not Peter — then they can deal with it appropriately. Teachers can't make accusations either, but could arrange to check other classes' bags if it happens again."

Airlie worried all night about what she would say to Mr Rodgers. But in the end, it was pretty painless.

"Mr Rodgers, can I talk to you for a couple of minutes before class?" Airlie tried to keep her voice light but serious.

"Certainly, why don't we go into the classroom and we can talk while I get ready for class?" Mr Rodgers unlocked the door and let her in.

"Why isn't the classroom locked at lunchtime, and in the breaks?" Airlie asked thoughtfully. "We're not allowed to stay in the classroom unless it's wet."

"Strictly speaking you aren't meant to be there, but in practice students often need to get to their bag to get a drink or put their lunchbox away. But that might change if the thefts continue."

"My brother told me that something similar happened in his homeroom."

"Yes, ours was the second incident. Did your brother have anything stolen?"

"Maybe a cricket ball... But he didn't notice it at the time, so it wasn't reported."

"So why are *you* talking to *me*?" Mr Rodgers queried with a raise of his eyebrow.

"Because I think I might have seen who did it. Last night I recalled someone who looked like he might have come out of our homeroom." Airlie said carefully.

"So where were you and what exactly did you see."

"I was skipping with my friends on the west lawn and noticed something out of the corner of my eye. I saw a chunky boy with light brown hair coming from direction of our homeroom, and I think he might have been in the classroom. I think what attracted my attention was him coming out of the room and pulling the door closed."

"Did you recognize who it was?"

"I thought I recognized him as a year 6 boy, but don't know his name. Though my brother thinks he might know him. But my mum says I should just say what I saw and nothing more."

"Wise advice... If you do see him again, go to the teacher on playground duty and point him out. I'll make sure the staff are all aware that we have a suspect."

For the next few days, Airlie was careful to keep an eye on where the duty staff member was as well as trying to be aware of the other classrooms. It seemed unlikely that he'd try for Peter's or hers again, at least not so soon. The teachers also seemed to be keeping a bit of an eye on her, and never wandered too far away.

Thursday lunchtime, she was in the air above the rope when she caught sight of someone coming out of a year 5 classroom. She stumbled a bit as she landed, twisting her ankle slightly.

"Sorry!" Airlie yelped to her surprised friends, as she hobbled over to the teacher on duty, Miss Lee.

Airlie deliberately didn't look straight at the chunky boy but rather at the teacher. "The boy I saw the other day is just coming from the year 5 classrooms. He came out of the one on the left."

Miss Lee swept her gaze around the playground, without lingering on the boy. "I see him. Why don't you sit down and rest your foot? You should go and see the school nurse if it's a problem. Don't walk on it unsupported."

Airlie sat down on the nearest bench and rubbed her ankle. It was a bit swollen, she thought. Lilly and Yan came and sat next to her.

"Is it bad?" Lilly asked. Airlie shook her head.

"Did Miss Lee say you should go to the office and get a bandage?" Yan asked. Airlie nodded, and her two friends helped her across the playground.

As they limped into the office, one of the office staff came over to help, and got her seated in a comfy chair with her foot elevated on a stool. After a quick round of explanations, she addressed Yan and Lilly: "Thanks for helping, girls. There's no need to wait. The bell's about to go and you should get to class. The nurse is looking after someone else right at the moment, but won't be long."

The bell went while they were filling in some forms, noting details about the incident and excusing her from class while it was dealt with.

Just as they finished, a skinny boy emerged from the clinic bringing a scent of antiseptic and sporting large bandaids on

18

his left elbow and over his left eyebrow. "Tennis ball soccer," he mumbled to her without meeting her eyes.

"I hope the tennis ball got what it deserved," Airlie whispered to his back. He hesitated a moment, but didn't turn around.

As the nurse ushered Airlie in, a breathless runner came in reporting another theft — from a year 5 homeroom. As the door was closed behind her, Airlie closed her eyes and stretched her senses to hear the details: they were going to get all the year 5 and year 6 students to turn out their bags.

Airlie was just coming out of the infirmary, testing out her ankle with its supporting bandage, when the office door opened and Chunky was marched in by a teacher, who threw down a bag. "Is the principal around? I have an update on the robberies. Everything that was taken today seems to be in this bag, plus several things from the earlier robberies."

From the corner of her eye, Airlie noted the principal and the vice-principal emerge from their offices, but her focus was on the bag as she approached. "Theft not robbery," she murmured. "There was no violence involved."

Then at full volume she continued, pointing into the bag, "But that's *my* pencil case with the black cat stickers."

Chunky seemed to shrivel under Airlie's glare.

A ball raced across the playground followed by a horde of boys. Sooty tensed in her lap, as if ready to pounce, but Airlie stroked him firmly from head to tail as she rewound the scene in her mind.

She had seen the boy from sickbay, but he wasn't playing soccer: he'd just put his lunch wrapper in the bin and been blindsided as the game swerved out of its ill-defined boundaries.

Dad had an 'eidetic' memory that allowed him to see and describe things in detail even though he'd only glimpsed them for a fraction of a second. He said it was much stronger when he was a boy, but still he could describe scenes from his youth with photographic detail, and could visualize the exact page of a book he'd read years ago and tell you exactly where on the page a particular word was. He could do that for things he'd read recently too, or even with just a quick skim of the newspaper.

He just looked for words or pictures of interest, knowing he could review the details at leisure if he was interested.

What Airlie was doing seemed to be different: it wasn't just a photographic memory of a scene or a page. It wasn't even just that she could page back and forth like in a book, or rewind and fast-forward like a video. Somehow, she could adjust her perspective too, see things better from a different point of view. Dad said that was 'reconstruction', and Mum said that almost all our memories were actually reconstructions and amalgamations based on a bit of detailed information about the particular event and a lot of experience of similar events.

As Dad was a neuroscience professor and Mum was a practising psychologist, they should know what they were talking about. But Airlie wasn't convinced by their explanations.

Chapter 2

"... and I told them 'Airlie got a cat for her birthday because she promised to do all the work looking after it' and they said 'There's a lot more work with a dog, and you've got to get it trained' and I said 'There's a trainer advertised on the noticeboard at the pound and they have classes on Saturday afternoon at the park and it's only half my pocket money for the weekly lessons and it's only for ten weeks and there's poodles just been weaned at the pound and it's one of the best dogs for allergies and I put my name on the waiting list and there's one that I really like and they'll only keep it for me till tomorrow.'"

Yan stopped for a breath and the puppy on the leash yapped happily in agreement, and Airlie finally got a word in after the girls had been dragged about a block and a half from her house. "That's great! Obviously, they gave in after all those years of high-pressure tactics... What's his name?"

"Nonsense!"

"Nonsense?" Airlie tried to keep her tone neutral, but felt it was a typical Yan kind of name.

"Well my dad suggested 'Nuisance', but Mum always said we wanted a 'no nonsense' dog and when I remembered how he reacted to the keeper at the pound saying that... Well, I'll show you."

They'd stopped and the puppy was nosing around in some weeds when Yan spoke sharply to it, saying "No Nonsense!" It immediately stopped what it was doing and looked around at her.

"I tried other names like Rover and Fido and Pluto, but Nonsense is the one he responds to best — just like at the pound."

Yan steered them right again, and they quickly approached her house. Yan explained. "At this stage I'm only meant to be walking him for five minutes, but each week a puppy can do an extra minute, which is about an extra block. Eventually we'll be able to do walks of half an hour morning and afternoon, and some longer walks on the weekends."

After a few weeks, the girls had managed to explore much of their suburb together, Airlie accompanying Yan and Nonsense in the mornings, and Lilly going with them in the afternoons, except that on Saturdays they all went to Nonsense training. That was sometimes a bit confusing because some of the other kids were impressed by how well Nonsense responded and tried the 'No Nonsense' command on their dogs.

Eventually Nonsense started to learn some obedience, and in particular learned to pay attention to whoever was holding her leash (or her treats) and not to be distracted by other people. He also learned to play ball and to fetch sticks, and could catch them high in the air.

But the funniest thing was when they put the ball on top of a bin while they picked up his 'business'. Nonsense started boinging into the air, with all four legs going like springs or pistons or something: boing, boing, boing... Airlie wondered if there was some kangaroo or springbok in his not-so-pedigree ancestry.

Although the bin was up to Airlie's shoulders, Nonsense was able to boing high enough to see the ball on the bin, but not enough to get it. And he didn't really try to jump up onto the bin.

Bin boinging became part of their regular Nonsense exercise routine, along with fence post and post box boinging since they were more common on their walks.

One Monday morning as they were extending the explorations into new territory (duly marked by Nonsense) they noticed a reward poster on a power pole (duly being marked by Nonsense). It was for $1000 and had a beautiful picture of a missing dog, a Pomeranian called Luna. Shortly afterwards they saw another poster on a gate post (duly being boinged as they read) and recognized that it was the actual address that the Pomeranian had disappeared from.

The dog had been missing since yesterday, but since the notices were still up it must still be missing. Airlie took pictures of the house and the poster and Yan put the phone number in her phone under Pomeranian, just in case they caught sight of it. "It's probably a pedigree dog," she commented as she took in the beautiful house and garden, and inspected the secure-seeming gate.

"That's good! They hopefully aren't interested in no-pedigree pound dogs with a bit of jackrabbit," Yan responded, taking the ball off the gate post and releasing Nonsense from boinging to a bit of fence sniffing.

"So you think it's been stolen too! It does seem rather too secure for a small dog to escape. Even a kangaroo-poodle hybrid would have trouble with that fence."

As if to confirm their suspicions, Nonsense stopped sniffing around the fence and howled at the gate as if he knew something was wrong. He started boinging to look over the gate into the yard.

"Yes, there's a dog living here," Yan told him. "Although maybe not anymore."

Airlie thought it noteworthy that all of Nonsense's energy was directed inside the gate. He hadn't seemed to pick up any interesting scent outside the fence. Yan called him down and crouched to calm him, caressing his ears and massaging his head and chucking him under the chin — and receiving a bath's worth of licks in return.

"It would be easy to take a dog," Yan continued. "I can imagine him yapping at the gate and then simply being bundled into a van or something."

Airlie talked about it with Sooty that night. They hadn't seen anything of the Pomeranian on their walk back this morning, and nor had Yan and Lilly this afternoon.

She thought back to yesterday, and mentally retraced their route. But if it was stolen yesterday, it was probably later in the day. Airlie's mind seemed to wind forward. The postman, would he have seen anything? She visualized the scene and wondered if the Pomeranian's owners had thought to ask the postman. In her mind, the front door was open but the screendoor was closed, and the little dog was yipping around the mailbox as the postman leant over the fence to put in the letters. There was also a red pillar box at the next corner. That would have been cleared around midday.

There would have been other delivery trucks, and Airlie had an impression of what they'd have looked like. She imagined the red postal van, a white delivery van, and a green removalist truck. She dismissed the postal van and the removalists quickly, but her thoughts remained on the delivery van for a while, and her imagination fleshed it out. Instead of having windows at the back it had blank panels. That would be perfect for holding a stolen dog.

Then there would have been children going to school and coming home again, paying more attention to each other than to their surrounds. In Airlie's mind, the dog was inside watching through the screendoor as the children went past yesterday morning. But no children left that house. And in the afternoon, there seemed to be no sign of the dog.

Airlie wondered if she knew any of the kids that walked past there. She knew that most of the students from her school lived in her suburb, and that some came from the southern parts where the dog had disappeared. She dug further into her memory and brought forward some faces that seemed to be likely prospects.

Likely prospects? I guess I'm going to play detective again tomorrow and see if any of those kids have seen anything. Maybe I should let the teachers know that there is a pedigree dog missing, presumed stolen, in the area.

There would be other families walking dogs in the area too.

★ ★ ★ ★ ★

In the morning, Yan and Airlie went out early with Nonsense and Lilly, and Airlie messaged back and forth for a while and, after parking Nonsense back at Yan's, the three girls met up and traipsed through the school grounds to the south gate alongside the sportsfield. They talked to lots of kids and showed them pictures of the house and the poster on their phone, zooming in on the Pomeranian.

But none of them had seen anything suspicious, although some had noticed the poster and a couple students recognized the place and remembered the dog yapping away at the screendoor in the mornings.

Miss Lee was on playground duty as they headed back towards their homeroom, and when they showed her the poster, she thought it would be a good idea to let the office take a copy — and maybe the deputy principal would make an announcement about it.

The office manager, Miss Phillips, was sympathetic but thought they should ring the owner for more details and make sure the dog hadn't been found yet. She dialled the number and after identifying herself and the school, passed the phone to Airlie to talk about what they'd been doing to help. Meanwhile Miss Phillips took the picture off Airlie's phone and printed it, taking it into the vice-principal's office just as the bell rang.

During the announcements, Miss Phillips wrote out a late chit for Airlie and her friends, but to her surprise Airlie got a mention. "If anyone has any information about the missing Pomeranian there will be a copy of the poster on the noticeboard outside the office, and Airlie Sanderson from 5A will be happy to meet you there at recess and exchange information."

Yan grabbed Airlie's arm and whispered in her ear as they left the office. "What did they say? Apart from talking about what we'd been doing all you seemed to say was things like 'Oh!' and 'You're Welcome!'"

"Well, I spoke to Mrs Furnsey, and Mr and Mrs Furnsey live on their own now their daughter's moved out. The daughter, Alison, actually gave them Luna as a kind of house-cooling gift to keep them company now she's gone. But Alison actually rang the council and other animal shelters and did the poster and put Luna on the missing pets website. And the website said they maybe shouldn't offer a reward because of scams, but they did anyway. And there's been no sightings or useful information yet, and ours was the first call."

"Oh, I'd forgotten about the reward," Lilly exclaimed. "We're not doing it for the reward, are we?"

Recess came and went, and apart from a few minutes with Yan and Lilly before they went off for a toilet break, Airlie had seen no one and had tried to concentrate on a short story she was reading on her phone.

A couple of minutes before the bell was due to ring, Airlie pocketed her phone and turned to go, but she heard a voice behind her: "Are you Airlie?"

The boy looked a bit younger than her, with a pale complexion supplemented by lots of freckles and a mess of vivid red hair. "Yes," she answered shortly, knowing the bell was about to go.

"Sorry, I couldn't get here earlier," he said in answer to her obvious displeasure and haste to get to class. "I got kept in. I'm Frank, Frank Lee!"

"So Frank, did you see something to do with the missing Pomeranian?" Airlie asked, trying to keep her voice light and polite.

"Yes... no... maybe..."

Airlie remained quiet and simply waited for more.

"It was not so much what I saw as what I heard. There was this van that passed me, and I heard barking from inside. Yapping really... sharp yipping. It sounded like a small dog. I don't know if it's got anything to do with your stolen dog though."

"We don't know it was stolen yet, but that does sound like there might have been a stolen dog inside, so we'll assume that for now. Were you near the crime scene or near the school? Or..."

"Maybe halfway between: still a few blocks from the school and about a block from the main road. They'd pretty well have to come that way if it was them."

"Hmm! What can you tell me about the van?" Airlie asked.

"It was like white, and I couldn't see in." Frank replied.

"Why couldn't you see in?"

"Well instead of windows it had blank panels: a panel van I guess."

"So was it big or small? Was it more like a car or more like four-wheel-drive or more like a truck?"

"Like a bit bigger than a car but smaller than a minibus, just a typical delivery van. It wasn't like a jeep or a truck or anything." Frank was interrupted by the bell going, and started to turn.

"Just a sec... Did you see the number plate or the make or any writing on it?"

"No writing, except I think it might have been a Ford. And I don't remember the number plate, except it was a bit different with two letters then two numbers then two letters. I remember the first two were BB. I thought it was cute."

"OK, well you'd better get to class. You don't want to get kept in again." Before he could turn away again, she handed him a bit of paper. "Here's my number."

As she hurried to class, Airlie wondered if Frank was related to Miss Lee. She was the teacher that had been on duty when she saw Chunky and hurt her ankle. But then Lee or Li, whichever it was, was a very common Asian name — like Smith and Jones — though Frank didn't look Asian.

Just as she was getting to class a message came in. She pulled out her phone and saw that it was from Frank. *Good, I can get in touch if I think of anything else to ask.*

That evening, Sooty was snoozing on Airlie's lap as she sat in a recliner trying to get through her story before dinner. But she kept thinking of the Pomeranian and the white panel van. Frank's description matched very well to the van she'd imagined last night.

Finishing the story, she put down her phone and Sooty took the opportunity to push her head into her hand. She lay back and closed her eyes, allowing her thoughts to wonder back to the yapping dog and the white van. *BB99AA*, she thought BB followed by two digits followed by two letters. Her dad had once mentioned to her that there was an old programming language where you put a 9 for unknown digit and an A for an unknown letter. But she couldn't superimpose that on the fuzzy numberplate in her mind.

She swung her attention around to the front of the van, trying to catch a glimpse of the driver, but he had a green baseball cap pulled low over his eyes and his face was in shadow. But there was a silhouette behind him, a passenger.

But the numberplate caught her attention. She could see BB93, but the rest was still blurry. The three was a bit like a 9 but with a bit missing, or like an 8 with two bits missing. But why was she seeing it as a 3?

Airlie swung her vision up to look at the passenger. She could barely make him out through the windscreen, but she could see that he was wearing dark sunglasses and his hair seemed quite light, blond maybe. Suddenly it seemed a bit sunnier, and as the van turned a corner she noticed the back numberplate: BB93CA.

But was that really a 9 and an A, or did it mean that her dream number was still missing a digit and a letter?

Airlie sat up and reached for her phone and sent Frank a text.

'Did you see anything of the driver? Was there a passenger? Airlie'

Then a moment later, she messaged:

'Think about the digits, try putting the numbers 1, 2, 3, … in and seeing if they seem to fit your memory. Then for the last two try letters, A, B, C,…'

A message came back as she was hitting send:

'Yeah, the driver was wearing a green cap. I wouldn't recognize him. The passenger maybe looked like a surfie: yellow-blond hair, sunglasses you know.'

Then a minute later, 'Oh yeah, I do remember that the letters were all from the beginning of the alphabet, but only the two Bs so BB..AC or BB..CA.'

'What about the digits? Were they all from the beginning, like 123 or the end like 789?'

'Both maybe. Like I thought that it just missed out being 123, maybe there was a 3. But the other one couldn't have been more different, like 0 or 9.'

'Thanks Frank. That really helps. I'll pass on the information.'

Wow! thought Airlie. *That's all consistent with my imagined scene, like a vision. Even the number BB93CA.*

But that's impossible… And who do I pass the information on to anyway?

After dinner, Airlie searched the police website. As well as the emergency and crime reporting numbers, there was an anonymous whistleblower number and a potentially nonymous (*is that even a word?*) web contact form.

Airlie chose to put her first name, and her class and school address. She wasn't allowed to put her full name or her address on the web because her mum said there were predators out there. The police should be okay, but this way they'd have to talk to her at school if they wanted to.

The first part was easy: them walking the dog and seeing the missing dog posters and then talking to Mrs Furnsey about Luna, and the school making her the liaison for any information the students had.

The second part was not so easy: they'd think she was a crank if she started talking about visions. So she wrote this part very diplomatically. And she included the messages to and from Frank word for word. Then she finished off very carefully.

'I didn't see the van personally at that time, and don't really remember seeing it in the neighbourhood. But perhaps I did because it seems a bit familiar. Anyway, for whatever reason, whatever I'm remembering, the license number might be BB93CA.'

Airlie, Yan and Lilly were sitting in homeroom spread across the front row, Airlie's mind as usual half on the announcements and half on other things. But then Yan nudged Airlie, and she dredged from her brain the last few words out of the loudspeaker. The three of them had been asked to report to the office immediately.

There was a man in a neat suit waiting for them. He introduced himself as Inspector Humble, and gave them each a card. It said Inspector Jonathan Humble, Minor Cases.

Airlie took a quick look at it, and opened her mouth before remembering not to put her foot in it. "Is that minor in the sense of unimportant, or minor in the sense of children?"

Inspector Humble didn't seem to mind. If anything, he seemed amused. "Yes and no," he replied. "There's no such thing as unimportant cases, but yes sometimes there is a sense of them being less important cases. However, it is deliberately ambiguous because you are absolutely correct, we deal with cases that involve minors either as victims, or witnesses or suspects. And really, whenever there are children involved we regard them as especially important cases. But, of course, the criminals we are interviewing don't generally tumble to that."

The inspector explained that he wasn't going to interview them formally: if that were necessary it would require their parents' involvement. But today it was just "an informal exchange of information" with the Vice-Principal present as a witness or chaperone or something. He talked to Lilly first, so she could get back to class and then Yan who had been a bit more involved. Then he asked about Frank and because there were several Franks, the Vice-Principal asked her to pick him out of last year's class photos, but she already remembered his surname was Lee — so that was easy. The Vice-Principal leaned out the door for a moment to ask Miss Phillips to get him.

The Vice-Principal seemed to shift about uncomfortably when she talked about thinking or daydreaming about the house and the van and the number plate. But Inspector

Humble seemed quite unperturbed. "Our psychologists keep on telling us that the mind, and memory, work in mysterious and not always logical ways. But that doesn't make dreams or mixed memories irrational. It is just a different kind of rationality. The brain associates different things, and it is very hard to get a pure witness recollection that hasn't been influenced by previous events or other factors."

Airlie was still a little concerned after that. "That doesn't mean that I'll have to see a psychiatrist or anything does it?"

"I wouldn't think so. It is very unlikely that you'll be called as a witness as you really didn't witness anything directly, although we can arrange a session with a Police Psychologist if it would seem helpful. And there is clearly something to your memories as there is a white Ford panel van with plates BB93CA. There are other officers following up on that as we speak."

There was a tap on the door and Miss Phillips stuck her head around. "Frank Lee is here. Do you want..."

"Yes, show him in please Miss Phillips," the Vice-Principal interrupted. "We don't want to keep him away from class too long."

Frank came into the room and gave Airlie an uninterpretable look. He was probably not happy about being brought before the vice-principal. Just wait till he learns it's an interview with the police.

But Inspector Humble was quite disarming. "Frank, pleased to meet you. I just wanted to thank you for your assistance on behalf of the police. Also, if I can have your phone number and your parents' numbers that would be very helpful. We may need to be in contact again. Also, I need to inform you that Airlie has shared your text messages with us, and we will be seeking to get a copy of your interactions from the phone company just for the record. Can you let me have the exact times of the messages you sent and received please?"

The inspector could have got Frank's phone number and message times from Airlie, but he wrote down the details Frank gave him and said he could go.

That evening there was a phone call for Airlie on her mobile that came just as Inspector Humble was talking to her parents on the landline. She answered it as she went up to her room.

"Airlie, it's Irene Furnsey here," said a breathless voice. "It's Luna. They found her. She's home. Say hello to Airlie, Luna." There was a yap, a pause, and then yip-yap.

"Pleased to meet you Luna, glad to hear you're home safely. Can you put me back to Mrs Furnsey please?"

"Oh Airlie," said a now sobbing voice. "The police just found her and brought her back. The inspector said that you and your friends had provided the information that led to capture of the dognapping ring. Apparently, there were seven pedigree dogs recovered and all of them have rewards."

"But I didn't do it for the reward. It was just... I was worried about Luna. We just wanted to help."

"Well, the police will be in touch with your parents about the rewards. I just wanted to invite you and your parents and your friends — and your friend's dog — around for afternoon tea on Saturday. Can you let me know?"

Chapter 3

Airlie's reputation as a girl detective and problem solver grew quickly, with Yan known as her sidekick. But it wasn't really that she was a good detective, or particularly perceptive… just that she had this strange ability to imagine things from different perspectives, to see things that she hadn't exactly seen. And her visual memories continued to deliver unexpected viewpoints.

In the last week of term, Airlie and Yan were once again called to the office. There were raised eyebrows, rolled eyes and soft mutters of "not again", but Airlie and Yan left without a word until they were outside the classroom.

"But you haven't had a case in weeks," Yan said.

"I can't think of anything they'd want to see us about either," answered Airlie. "Maybe there's something new they'd like us to look into."

"But teachers wouldn't, couldn't, ask students to play detective, could they, would they?"

"Well, we'll know soon enough," Airlie replied as they approached the office.

Vice-Principal Dexter was there talking to Mrs Fenster, and quickly directed them into the same small meeting room where they'd met Inspector Humble. Mrs Fenster was the school guidance counsellor and had talked to them once about career opportunities, and subject choice in high school. But normally she only had one-to-one meetings with Year 6 students — and even then, not with the vice-principal present.

Mrs Fenster had them sit, then jumped right into it. "Airlie, there are a couple of opportunities that have come up for you, and Yan might be interested too as I know that she has, uh, helped you solve a few mysteries. The first is a new summer program introduced by the police, the Department of Minor Affairs."

"Oh, so it's an invitation from Inspector Humble from Minor Cases is it?"

"Yes, I understand he's involved. They are organizing a summer camp for middle grade students interested in police work. It will involve both physical and mental training, learning about police procedure, and so on, and there will also be a variety of camp activities: swimming, hikes, archery, shooting, campfires and such like. And you've been offered a free place."

Airlie wasn't sure what she thought, particularly about the physical training. But it could be fun. But Yan squeaked with excitement. "Wow! That sounds great. But it seems like I'm not being offered a free place, and maybe Lilly would be interested too. We normally spend most of the summer together."

"The school has also been offered some discount places, and we wanted to offer you one of those, Yan, and..." Mrs Fenster looked across at the vice-principal, who nodded almost imperceptibly. "We should be able to offer one to Lilly too if she was interested. Inspector Humble was very keen for you and Airlie to attend."

"I don't know," responded Airlie thoughtfully. "I hadn't really considered the police as a career... I'd been more thinking about being a scientist, a biologist maybe, a neurologist... or perhaps a psychologist. But forensics might be a possibility: I enjoy those shows."

"Yes, well many of the career opportunities in the police force require a degree, and yes forensics of every kind is very important and does require at least a bachelor's degree, and police psychologists obviously need an appropriate degree too."

"And your interest in science relates to the other opportunity that has come up," inserted Vice-Principal Dexter. "You may have heard of the specialist Science and Mathematics high school. Next year they're introducing an Opportunity Class for Years 5 and 6. It will go through the normal curriculum in an accelerated way while giving you the opportunity to undertake tasters of various areas of science from bioinformatics to quantum psychology."

Mrs Fenster handed each of them a copy of a glossy brochure about the program, explaining more as she did so. "It is very competitive, only 30 places each for the whole state. There is a placement test, and any Year 4 or Year 5 student can apply, but there is also a component of the score that is based on the school assessment across English, Mathematics and Science. You two have the top scores for our Year 5, and should be quite competitive."

"Err, that sounds quite interesting," mumbled Airlie.

"But what about Lilly?" grumbled Yan.

"Here is another brochure for her," Mrs Fenster responded, handing it to Yan. "But Lilly hasn't performed as well as you two, so would have to do very well on the test. Still, this is part of what you will all want to talk about with your parents. We are sensitive to your friendships and the social aspects of your decision. Indeed, part of the point of the program is to place you with other high-achieving science-oriented students and allow you to develop significant relationships with your peers. Even if some of you don't get in, just because you are going to different schools doesn't mean you can't still be friends."

PART TWO

CAMP

Chapter 4

"Welcome to Camp Polis! My name is Jonathan Humble, Camp Director. Some of you have already met me in my official role as Inspector in the Minor Crimes division. Many of you will be wondering why we had you and your parents sign a confidentiality agreement in relation to what you learn at this camp. As far as your parents and outsiders are concerned, this is because we will be talking about actual police procedures, including matters that we hope will not become known to the criminal fraternity for some time. But right now, I want to talk about some of the more unique aspects that fall under this policy, and indeed your special gifts are regarded as matters of national security."

A boy Airlie's age or slightly older put his hand up and the inspector acknowledged him.

"What if some of our family are criminals? How do you know you aren't letting the cat out of the bag?" he asked.

"Some of you have got up to some mischief! As for your families, we vetted them very thoroughly, but still we ask you to use discretion about the things we learn here."

Humble hesitated for a moment as he touched something on his laptop. "Some of you will want to discuss certain things with your parents. Some things you may decide you shouldn't discuss. And I would suggest you tell your Uncle Mario as little as possible.

That caused chuckles all round, but Arlie noted that the boy himself was looking shocked rather than amused. The inspector didn't seem to notice either, but attempted another little joke: "As for cats and bags, I hope you are enjoying our pet friendly facility, and that you and your pets have settled in well."

Airlie put her hand up, and asked. "Why is it called Camp Polis? Polis means city and that seems strange for a camp located in the middle of a national park!"

"Now that's a good opportunity for a sidetrack." Humble grinned before continuing. "We can't afford to get bogged down with irrelevant questions, and some questions I won't be able to answer. So Sergeant Harry Marks will note down questions that we can't deal with here and now."

He indicated to the side where the sergeant raised his hand in response.

"Furthermore, there is a letterbox at the back in the doorway through to the mess hall. Questions and comments can be placed in there at any time — anonymous if you like. You are encouraged to make note of any questions or ideas that you have."

While people looked around to see the question box, Humble glanced down at his laptop and touched the screen again. Airlie wasn't interested in the locked box that she'd noticed coming in, but her eyes roved over the forty or fifty kids around her — with girls in the clear majority, maybe two-thirds.

"As for your question, Miss Sanderson..." Airlie jumped in shock as he looked straight at her, "This is more than a camp, it is a fort! And although *polis* classically meant city/state, its original meaning *was* more like 'fort'. Our security is high, with video surveillance and face identification employed at the perimeters and around the camp. It is also related to certain very relevant words like 'politics' and 'police' in the same way that the word 'city' connects etymologically to 'civil' and 'civilization'. So yes, a good sidetrack, but one that leads me to touch on some important aspects of our program here."

There was a lot of murmuring and movement at the mention of surveillance, but Airlie had spotted the cameras as she came in, so kept her gaze on the platform where Inspector Humble met it evenly. Maybe he hadn't remembered her name but had picked it up from his surveillance monitor. However, as he met her eyes, she was sure he had really recognized her.

Police have to be good at that sort of thing.

He was still looking at her as he started to speak again.

"You may be aware that we are near the hadron collider here. That is not a coincidence. Camp Polis is located within the collider security precinct and there are places you will not be allowed to wander. Furthermore, the reason why you are here is closely related to the collider. The fact that you have been offered places in opportunity classes featuring quantum physics and quantum psychology is also related to this. And if you haven't accepted, it is not too late to change your mind at the end of the camp. The unusual gifts and increased brain activation that you and your friends and your pets seem to have *are* a major part of the story, and the primary grounds for various confidentiality agreements associated with Camp Polis and the Department of Minor Affairs."

Pandemonium broke out.

You mean I'm not the only one with strange visions! Maybe the other kids and pets have real superpowers, like in the movies...

Inspector Humble seemed to have expected the reaction. He let it run for a minute then banged a gavel or something and reclaimed everyone's attention.

"In terms of your accommodation, we have grouped you into cabins with people with different manifestations of the quantum gift, rather than others with a similar ability. In addition, your duty roster is organized by cabin and posted in your cabins, so you'll be spending most of your time in these groups. We want you to learn and explore how *different* abilities relate. Can your various talents work together? Are they indeed manifestations of a single gift that represents further abilities that you yourself could master?"

Humble glared around the room, seeming to catch everyone's eyes for a moment.

"With talents comes responsibility. We will not tolerate any bullying or hazing or insolence, and we have assigned a sergeant to each cabin to advise you and keep order. That is not to say that they are there to keep you out of mischief. In fact, some of them might even show you how it's done properly." His eyes flicked across to Sergeant Marks, who spread his hands and raised his eyebrows in a smirking show of innocence.

Airlie, Yan and Lilly had been assigned to a cabin with five other girls and a Sergeant Eleanor (*call me El*) Sanford. The cabin sported its own amenities with triple showers, double sinks and a couple of separate toilets. The dorm had four double bunks and Airlie and Yan had claimed head-to-head top bunks with Lilly taking the one under Airlie. Another group of three girls did much the same, and the last two girls got adjacent bottom bunks. Airlie's explorations determined that there was a separate room for the sergeant who had a queen bed all to herself, plus an ensuite. Most importantly, there was also a pleasantly scented room with litter trays, water bowls, scratch poles, and plenty of room for travel cages for the four cats and a rabbit. The room next to that had a backdoor with a pet flap out into a meshed-in run for the two dogs.

Amazingly, there weren't any savage run-ins between the animals, although Sooty seemed to stick to her plastic travel cage. Normally she hated it because it meant she was going to the vet.

Lilly was the only girl in their cabin who hadn't brought a pet, but she *had* rescued a large brown spider from another girl, Wendy, who had screamed and was about to go after it with a slipper. After a few minutes in residence in Lilly's tooth glass, she got permission from El to let it go outside in the brush.

The previous night after the welcome talk, they'd been bundled off to bed quickly without much time to connect names to faces, and now at dawn they were being hauled out of bed for a run — camp uniforms provided in the correct sizes! Different levels of fitness quickly split up the original cliques. But as Airlie and Lilly weren't as fit as Yan, they found themselves competing for last place with a couple of their other bunkmates.

El had been waxing enthusiastically about the wide variety of trails around the camp, pointing to a green trail marker as she explained they were taking an easy circular route that was fairly flat and only 2 k's. But that was about all Airlie heard before she fell back out of earshot.

Airlie and her companions managed to get their names straight between puffs as they watched the other girls spread out ahead of them, Yan running easily at El's elbow, with Nonsense at their heels, and Wendy and her black labrador not far behind, and the two other girls jogging comfortably together a little further back.

By the time they got back to their cabin, the four girls in the rearguard were just walking and talking, and Airlie and Lilly were getting on well with their new friends Sandy and Georgie. Airlie didn't normally make friends easily, but somehow she felt relaxed. Maybe it was the cool of the early morning and the hints of pine in the air.

Georgie insisted that she didn't have any special powers, but that sometimes Sandy seemed a bit telepathic, which is probably why she caught their names more quickly than vice versa. The rabbit was called Miffy and was Georgie's, while Sandy had brought her calico cat Cleo. Remembering how Nonsense was tagging along with Yan, they laughed at the idea of having cats and rabbits running on leads during their morning jog and then turned to a more serious discussion about why they had to bring their pets and how they were going to fit into camp life.

That question was soon answered. Breakfast was waiting for them, thanks to El and Yan, and they had a couple of visitors — one in a keeper's uniform whom Airlie recognized from the pound where Yan had got Nonsense. Tony, his name was.

"Oh, no thank you," Tony was saying. "We've already had breakfast." But giving the lie to his words, he snaffled a bit of still sizzling bacon, popped it in his mouth then licked his fingers and puffed and panted to cool his mouth. "Nice and hot," he commented amidst this, somehow managing a grimace that again belied his words.

Clearly, the animals were tied to the strange gift phenomenon, and Tony referred to them in witchy terms as *familiars*, but was chided quite severely about that by the woman in the dress suit, a Dr Eerdmann, who was apparently a famous animal psychologist. They were part of a team of a dozen animal specialists ranging from academics to zookeepers, not to mention several representatives from the police dog squad — complete with their canine counterparts.

Just to get started, they were going to be training their cats, rabbits, hamsters and guinea pigs to walk on leads, and the dogs not to eat them!

Oh! And the fact that the animals had got on so well the previous night was no accident. Tony explained that the sweet-smelling pet rooms were due to special concoctions of scents and pheromones designed to ensure they were relaxed and happy together. They also hoped that the *familiar* bonds and a bit of training would help them avoid nasty incidents.

Chapter 5

Airlie stood in front of their dorm's roster and took it in. Interestingly there was no spud-bashing, bean-peeling or the like. The only meal they were expected to manage for themselves was breakfast, and that was itself meant to be a learning experience: they were expected to do their own cooking and their menu would vary from bacon and eggs to pancakes with toppings of their choice. Or according to their ability!

There were, of course, normal camp activities with archery and airgun ranges, woodcraft and canoeing, and the expected campfire cum barbecue. But in addition, there were sessions with various police officers, animal handlers, psychologists, and scientists — plus a visit to the hadron collider.

Animal training was next, and for this they combined with some other cabins and were allocated amongst the trainers according to their kind of pet. Dogs and cats were in the majority, but there were a variety of other animals and those without one were allocated to the dog squad to see if they could connect with one of their puppies.

But Lilly didn't seem to know what to do, and was looking around guiltily.

"What's up Lilly? Why aren't you heading over to find yourself a puppy?" Airlie asked.

"Actually, I think I've already found an animal companion," Lilly responded, stretching out her arm to show a mysterious lump moving along the bottom of her sleeve. "I call him Parker because I found him parked on my pillow this morning. I did think of Peter, but I wasn't sure it was a 'he' — though for some reason I think it is."

Airlie gasped as a large brown spider, emerged from Lilly's sleeve and climbed around onto her hand. Lilly brought it up level to her eyes and stared into Parker's two rows of four eyes set in a yellowish band around the top of his head. Sooty stretched up in his cage and peered at it.

A voice from behind her startled Airlie, "You're right, it's a male _Heteropoda venatoria_: a huntsman spider. You can tell by the creamy clypeus and carapace."

"Aren't they poisonous?" Airlie squeaked.

Tony walked slowly into view. "They certainly are venomous, although it's rare for a bite to be a problem for humans. Also, if you don't scare them, they won't bite. And this one's certainly taken a shine to your friend: I've never seen anything like it."

"Oh, sorry Tony! This is my friend Lilly. Lilly, this is Tony who works at the pound."

"In fact, that's just to earn a bit of pocket money. I'm a PhD student in Biology, and as it happens I have a particular interest in insects and arachnids, although my thesis is focussed on parasites. I didn't expect to find any familiars from the Arthropoda phylum though. And to bond with it in a single night too..." A touch of awe seemed to enter Tony's expression.

Lilly responded hesitantly. "Nice to meet you, Tony. Yes, it's very strange but there seems to be a connection. Even last night when I rescued him from Wendy, he seemed kind of friendly. But when I woke this morning, he was sitting on the pillow staring at me. And when I sat up, it seemed only natural for me to put down my hand for him to climb on to."

Tony's voice was a bit more assertive when he spoke again. "Yes, well you can join me and the other unusual critters, Lilly. But Airlie, you're holding up the cat group; and I can see your cat's looking a bit antsy."

"Oh! That's Sooty. Sooty meet Tony..." Airlie held up the pet carrier so they could get a quick look at each other.

Airlie hurried over to the group of kids with cat cages. A couple of handlers carrying leads were chatting quietly, when a voice rang out from one of the girls — Jen — from the same school as Wendy. "Here she is! Not only does she walk when she's meant to be running, and leave us do all the work for breakfast, she's holding us all up again now."

Airlie glanced at the time, but otherwise ignored her — except that Sooty set off a hissing match with Jen's cat as they passed her.

She was less than a minute late, and had a good excuse. Coming up beside Sandy, she exclaimed breathlessly, "Lilly's got a pet now. I hope her parents are okay with it."

"Oh! She bonded with a puppy, did she?" Sandy responded.

"No, not a puppy... Do you remember that huntsman spider she rescued from Wendy? Well, it came back in the night, and she woke up with it sitting on her pillow staring at her. She bonded a poisonous spider and keeps it up her sleeve."

"Oh! Still, I guess it's good to have some surprises up your sleeve."

"Ha! Ha!"

Just then a strong male voice overrode all the chitchat. "Hello everyone! Good to see you're all here promptly. I'm Mike and this is Pam. We're going to be working on getting your cats to walk nicely on leads, without getting distracted. And once that's working well, we'll see if your bond is strong enough to do it without the leads.

"But first," Pam put in, "we want to separate you two with the hissing toms." She pointed to Jen and swept her arm away from Airlie. "You four come with me, the rest can stay here with Mike."

Mike waited till Pam led her group behind the cabins, then gave Airlie and Sandy their leads. "You're Airlie Sanderson aren't you," he said as he handed hers over. She nodded automatically, but then stood there with a frown on her face until he explained. "I consult for the council and heard about your dognapping ring. And I was there for your question about the Camp Polis name."

Sandy snorted. "You didn't tell me you *ran* a dognapping ring," she accused.

Mike laughed merrily. "No, she and her cat used their superpowers to put away a dognapping ring. That's what gave the police the idea to have this camp for bonded kids. One of the gang had a sister who was a receptionist for a vet, and got the lowdown on the expensive dogs. They stole seven dogs from our council area, and others from neighbouring municipalities."

Sandy looked stunned for a moment, then put on the same accusing tone and the matching frown. "You didn't tell me you *caught* a dognapping ring!"

Chapter 6

"Hey Airlie, wait up!" Yan raced up to her, excited and panting — as did Nonsense. Yan put her hand on Airlie's shoulder, pulling her round. Nonsense put his paws on Airlie's knees and thighs, pulling her down.

Reaching out with one hand for Nonsense to lick, she then ruffled his head while she pulled Yan into a hug with her other arm, as much for balance as anything else.

"There was this girl at the dog group," Yan gasped out. "She reminded me of you. She's blind..."

"Wow! Well, *thanks* a lot Yan!" Airlie managed.

"No, I mean Kate's blind, but she's got a seeing-eye dog and it's like she can see through the dog's eyes or something. That's kind of like you, isn't it?"

"Oh! Well, thanks Yan! I guess you'll need to introduce me. I know they deliberately put us with people with different 'gifts'. But maybe it would make sense to get together with people with similar abilities. It seems like a missed opportunity. I might try and catch Inspector Humble and see if we can have a chance to get together with the kids most like ourselves."

"Actually, I've asked her to sit with us at lunch. Nobody said we had to stay in our cabin groups. And I think they're pairing us up with different cabins each day for the animal groups. So that will mean we eventually pair up with each cabin. We should make sure we share about our groups and compare gifts. C'mon!"

"How come you're so puffed anyway, Yan? You jogged a couple of k's earlier this morning without problem."

"Oh, they had us running around an obstacle course with our dogs. And then when I realized Kate was blind and what she could do, I just had to race back to tell you."

It took them a few minutes to get their pets settled in the cabin, and then Wendy and Lilly were back and the four of them set out for the mess together.

Wendy had met Kate and her golden labrador at the dog training, and her own chocolate labrador Cocoa had become great friends with Goldie. "Yes, very imaginative!" Yan commented before Airlie could.

Wendy spotted Kate coming out of a cabin with her dog in a harness, and called out to Goldie, racing over to greet her new friends. She stopped short when Kate said a firm "No!"

"No Wendy! When Goldie's wearing her jacket and harness, she's working and is not allowed to play. Please don't distract her or tempt her. It's okay to talk to me, but she's always got to be alert for dangers." She halted next to Wendy and Airlie, and Goldie stopped too, looking across at Airlie and sniffing faintly before turning to look around the camp.

"Oh! Sorry Kate!" Wendy apologized. "Anyway, you know Yan" — Goldie and Kate both looked towards Yan — "and this is Airlie" — Kate and Goldie both looked towards Airlie.

"Hi Kate and Goldie! Yan's told me a bit about you, and it seems we might have a similar gift." Kate and Goldie both seemed to meet Airlie's eyes.

"Great to meet you Airlie," Kate responded. "I'm hoping you'll be able to teach me some of your tricks. I can kind of see the world through Goldie's eyes now. But that's from where she is not from where I am. Yan says you can switch your perspective around even when your cat's not with you."

"Oh, it will so be exciting to share what I'm doing and see if you can do it too… Hopefully, I can give you some useful tips: I think in metaphors. At first it was like a video, fast-forwarding and rewinding, and then it was a bit more like a video camera, panning and zooming and stuff. Except that may not be very helpful for you… But now it's becoming more like navigating a web of possibilities of when and where someone might have been or might have gone: just following the threads — of whatever ideas I have — into imagined scenarios that turn out to be accurate. Which is all really quite confusing…"

Over lunch they practised, and Airlie tried to get Kate to shift her perspective up and down, and left or right. The problem was that Goldie was sitting between them and tended to move her head to look at things. Eventually, Airlie pushed back her chair and crouched down beside Goldie who looked deep into her eyes. She held the dog's head in her hands and spoke firmly. "Goldie, just stay like that and look at me! Don't look around at Kate! Don't look at what she's trying to look at! Do you understand?"

Kate looked straight at Airlie too, and nodded, but Airlie held Goldie's head firm. Then Kate looked down and screamed loudly enough to attract attention from nearby tables. "I did it! I managed to look down at Goldie and actually see *her*!"

Airlie let go of Goldie and edged back onto her chair. A moment later, Kate was even more excited when she managed to raise her perspective above Goldie's not very useful under-the-table world of smelly feet and knobbly knees! "Oh wow! I can see you all, and my food, and I can look around at each of you, and smell my own food." Kate reached over in front of Airlie for a jar of mustard pickles and took a deep sniff — which seemed to trigger an annoyed woof from under the table.

"Kate..." Airlie started, as she put the pieces together. "You share not just visual things with Goldie but smells. And it looks like you've brought his sense of smell up to the table too! You've had his sense of smelly feet, and now he is smelling your spicy pickles."

Wendy and Yan looked suitably amazed, but Kate seemed unphased. "Yes, I've noticed that I smell whatever Goldie's got her nose into, which can sometimes be quite yucky. Although she's very good at leaving things behind when I complain. But how is it that she's smelling what I'm smelling? It seems that somehow I'm shifting *her* sight and smell up at table level?"

Airlie watched Kate put the mustard down at arm's length and try to smell it long-distance by moving Goldie's senses into it. It was almost like she was being dragged along too. She shut her eyes, and suddenly she flipped into Kate's perspective, or rather Kate's version of Goldie's view, or something like that.

60

"Kate…" Airlie hesitated before continuing. "I think I can see through Goldie's eyes too. But the colour's all washed out. I'm not seeing proper reds or greens or purples." She kept her eyes shut and moved her hands around as if they were someone else's and, in washed-out Kate-Goldie mode, eventually managed to pick up in turn the tomato sauce, half a cucumber, and some sauerkraut. "The tomato sauce looks yellow, and the cucumber looks white: skin and all!"

"Oh Airlie, I never knew what to expect! I've always found talk of colours a bit confusing and then thought it wonderful, if still confusing, when I could see what Goldie sees. But I thought I just had to learn how to recognizes different colours and shades and things."

Yan piped up, commenting, "I'd always thought that dogs were colourblind."

"Technically they are, in that they don't have both red and green cones, but something that's kind of in between. And that fits: I'm seeing anything in the yellow to red range as yellow, while green is sort of cream. It must be resonating my blue cones too."

"Don't worry about Airlie! She goes all science nerd periodically!" Yan interjected.

But Kate took no notice. "How is that even possible? Goldie's under the table!" As Kate said that, Airlie's view suddenly shifted to a pair of crossed paws and sets of dirty feet in sundry footwear.

"Well… it's sort of like all the things I saw around town with Sooty's help when he'd never left the house."

"Sooty's Airlie's cat," Yan explained in case it wasn't obvious.

"What do you mean by 'resonating'?" Kate asked.

"Well, that's just my word for it!" Airlie shrugged. "Maybe we'll learn the proper words when we meet with the quantum physics and quantum psychology guys: there's things called quantum entanglement and quantum teleportation. But it seems to me that parts of my brain must be resonating with corresponding bits of Sooty's brain, and parts of your brain must be resonating with Goldie's brain — and now mine maybe. Except somehow we're resonating in other dimensions or something. Because we're seeing things that we're not in the right place to see. And in my case, mostly not even in the right time to see."

"You're doing the science nerd thing again Airlie," Yan pointed out.

"No I'm not! Any halfway decent Trekkie would understand all that!"

But Kate was already locked in her own world again, gazing around with an expression of wonder. "And for me it's smell too..." she murmured. "It's all so exciting! Maybe I can even learn to read actual books!"

"Does that mean that Goldie will have to learn to read?" Wendy wondered.

Chapter 7

Airlie was excited about the Quantum Psychology session, although in some ways she was disappointed that it wasn't Quantum Physics first, as she wanted to find out more about entanglement and twinning and teleportation.

Unfortunately, most of the stuff she could find online was either too complicated or too simplistic.

Airlie had been so buried in what she was digging into on her phone that she wasn't ready when the others headed off. But as she left the cabin, she could see them in front of her.

Airlie tapped her jeans pocket to make sure her phone was there, and wondered whether it was deliberate that they had good reception at the cabins and none in the main complex. Pulling out her phone again she saw she had some time, so she walked past the building and circumnavigated it checking how many bars she could get. Then she switched to a map to see where the reception shadow was in relation to the collider and the nearby township.

Maybe it was just that the cabins were nearer the town, or maybe when the collider was running maybe even that reception would drop out.

When she got to the meeting room, Yan and Lilly were sitting up the front at one table, with Wendy and a vacant chair at the next. "What happened to you?" she whispered as Airlie slipped into it.

But Airlie was distracted by the goodies on the table in front of them. It looked like a mix of cheap and expensive kit.

"Welcome to Quantum Psychology!" Prof. Freund was the very picture of a psychologist, complete with sharp grey beard and blue eyes piercing through the obligatory spectacles. He started by talking about the controversial nature of the field, and that different people meant different things by it, and that until now there was no empirical evidence behind any of the theories: some trying to explain consciousness or free will, others noting the similarity of various equations across the quantum and the neurological domains.

"But your extrasensory phenomena would seem to change all this. The most likely explanation seems to be that it relates to quantum effects triggered directly or indirectly by the collider experiments, but some suggest a role for dark matter or superstring theory. But then superstring theory, or M-theory, seek to reconcile all of Physics anyway, so perhaps it is a bit academic... Certainly as far as Psychology is concerned. We're hoping that some understanding of the science that might lie behind your gifts will help you develop new insights and capabilities, not to mention helping test the theories."

The professor paused to run his eyes around the group.

"The initial aim of these sessions is to understand what's happening to you in an empirical sense, it seems that somehow your nervous system has become entangled with that of your animal companion, and this seems to be mediated by entangled calcium ions. But we need empirical data to come up with better hypotheses and theories and predictions, and potentially some ideas about how to train quantum perception effectively."

Airlie put her hand up, and one of the tutors nudged the professor, who acknowledged her with a raise of an eyebrow. "Doesn't quantum entanglement refer to strictly twinned particles? That is exactly two particles at a time. How can it affect multiple people or animals at the same time?"

The professor raised his other eyebrow. "That's one of the things we are hoping to explore, and one of the reasons we have you in diverse groups. We expect that different pairings may be possible between different people and animals and sensoria, but not more than two at time. Or do you have some experience of something like that already? It seems to take weeks of exposure to the entangled milk products to produce an effect."

The animal psychologist they'd met earlier, Dr Eerdmann, gave Prof. Freund a sharp glare at that point, but he didn't seem to notice.

Airlie looked across at her friends, and shrugged.

"Do you know the blind girl, Kate, and her guide dog, Goldie? At lunch I was trying to help them change their perspective, and Kate was trying to project Goldie's olfactory senses at a distance, and somehow I was drawn into their shared view of the world — complete with the canine colour model."

The professor was quite taken aback and looked across at his colleagues. It was their turn to shrug.

So Airlie pushed on. "Also, it seems to take a matter of hours not weeks, but perhaps you can be presensitised.

Several people have made their connections here already. And I don't think milk can be the only factor, unless spiders drink milk."

This time Dr Eerdmann responded, smiling at her, clearly remembering her from earlier. "That's very interesting and we'll need to look into it. One of the aims we have here is to see if we can replicate the psychic phenomena under controlled conditions. But I think, Airlie, you'll need to tell us your spider story first."

"Oh no! That's not my story: it's Lilly and Parker's story."

As Lilly held out her hand and Parker climbed on to it, Airlie introduced them. "Meet Lilly and Parker."

Dr Eerdmann started, then stepped off the dais and leant forward warily to look at Parker. "Well now! I'll look forward to comparing notes with my animal behaviour colleagues when we meet this afternoon. But meanwhile Prof. Freund has some laboratory exercises for you to do."

Professor Freund took the hint, and started to explain about them doing a standard Brain Computer Interface experiment that they often did with kids at open days or school visits. Airlie recognized the newer Emotiv Brain Computer Interface kits with a hydrophilic gel electrode that conducted using sweat; she had the older version that was moistened with salt water. But this rig also included some comb-like electrodes with a separate electronics board — it didn't belong to the Emotiv kit.

She held it up and opened her mouth to ask about it, but Prof. Freund beat her to the punch. "In addition to the standard Emotiv BCI kit, we've also included a couple of research prototypes that connect to an OpenBCI board. This will give us additional information about the area associated with your dominant expanded abilities. Your demonstrator will help you connect them up and place them appropriately."

Normally the BCI experiment tracked your attention using a Visual Evoked Potential and then used this VEP to allow controlling a computer with your mind. But today it had an additional focus on making a connection to their pets. Still, some of the Professor's rambling comments and asides caught Airlie's attention.

Airlie was excited to hear that there was far more sophisticated high-density EEG, MEG and MRI equipment installed at the collider, and that there would be opportunities to follow up with higher resolution experiments using them, as well as being able to perform MEG and MRI on the animals.

She hardly listened to Professor Freund's careful explanation about participation being voluntary, or that they were here to receive appropriate training and assistance in developing their abilities in accord with the agreements their parents had signed.

Although she did note his emphatic declaration that it was *not* itself a research project. Apparently, the collider experiments had had unforeseen side-effects, so they were outside of the normal parameters of a research-oriented experiment, and they were concentrating on understanding and managing the effects. At this stage, all the known cases were south of the collider in the catchment area, and just half a dozen schools were involved.

With the help of Dr Eerdmann, set up went very quickly. The standard BCI task of trying to 'press' keys on a colourful grid of flashing letters by 'attending' to them was familiar. Last time it had been fun, but quite draining. This time, Airlie found it much easier.

Airlie and Sooty were paired with Wendy and Cocoa, to see if they could connect. Airlie went first, and also tried to get Sooty, Wendy's or Cocoa's perspectives of the screen. She reached out her mind to them in turn, but when that didn't work she and Sooty went behind the screen and she did that thing where she reoriented her imagined view to the screen and focussed on the virtual keys.

There was an awed "Wow!" from Wendy, and an excited clap from Dr Eerdmann who said something about 'scientific validation'. Although she managed to spell out more words quite easily, it really seemed to be just her usual mind trick and nothing to do with Wendy or Cocoa.

Airlie took off the EEG gear and helped Dr Eerdmann put it on Wendy and get set up again. This time she was to the side of the screen, holding Cocoa and directing him towards the screen both by holding his head gently and by closing her eyes and trying to sense his gaze. Suddenly, her vision washed out and she could see the screen, although the virtual keyboard was not much more than a blur of yellow. And, unfortunately, she wasn't wearing the EEG gear.

Suddenly she laughed, asking "Is there any particular reason you've used a red-green colour scheme for the letter grid? Because it won't work for colour-blind people, or dogs!"

Wendy realized instantly, complaining, "You've connected to Cocoa, and I've never been able to. How did you do it?"

Airlie moved behind Wendy and demonstrated on her. "I just held her head like this, looking at the screen, and then closed my eyes and concentrated." Suddenly the screen was in front of her closed eyes, in all its gory glory. She sent her attention slowly around the keyboard, typing: *Hi! This is Airlie!*

Silence overtook the entire room.

Chapter 8

Airlie and Kate agreed that archery sounded like fun, and rocked up in good time with Goldie. But for some reason the instructor, the aptly named Mr Fletcher, wouldn't let Kate shoot. Even Goldie seemed disappointed. After all, it was something like a throw and fetch stick game. And the fact that Kate was blind didn't really seem relevant anymore now that she could shift Goldie's viewpoint to her own.

Airlie followed the instructions carefully, putting on the protective gear then stringing her bow, and placing six arrows in an arrow stand at her feet. She drew the string back to her cheek and sighted on the bullseye — automatically fast forwarding to see how her shot would do.

She was going to overshoot the target.

"Don't hold it so long. You'll tire quickly. You need to learn to draw, aim and release in a single movement." Mr Fletcher instructed.

Airlie lowered her bow gradually until she could see the arrow hit the centre of the target, and released. Bullseye.

"Excellent Airlie! But pull back from the shoulder, not just the arm. Rotate your hips."

Airlie quickly repeated the steps with her remaining arrows. Six bullseyes — and several tingling muscles.

"Wow," said Kate. She and Goldie had been watching avidly, and Airlie suddenly switched to view the target through Goldie's eyes. She pulled Goldie's world to her own perspective, and then tried pushing it closer to the target.

"Right," announced Mr Fletcher. "Down bows. Everyone needs to fetch their arrows."

Kate and Goldie went with Airlie, and Kate pulled her perspective back to her as they reclaimed her arrows.

Soon they were ready to shoot another bracket, and this time Airlie pulled Goldie's view to her, noting that her blue-gold vision seemed somewhat crisper, and was quite suited to the target. She'd picked up on Goldie's nose as well and became hyperaware of the pine scent from the trees, as well as the smell of the freshly cut grass — plus various perfumes that did not come anywhere near to hiding the natural scent of the girls around her.

Kate and Goldie said nothing as they jointly loosed arrow after arrow. The first two were dead centre, but after that Airlie's shaking muscles seemed to pull them away into the second ring.

"Don't worry, you're doing remarkably well," Mr Fletcher reassured Airlie. "That's a fifteen-pound bow, and you'll need to work those muscles. It'll only take a few sessions before it's comfortable for half a dozen sets."

Kate was tickled pink as they walked away from the green. "What you did then, I can do, I'm sure!" she said.

Airlie nodded. Kate was using Goldie's view and was now able to look away from the path briefly. She was learning to look at people when she was talking to them. Picking up a nod was easy for her, although she still had difficulty with facial expressions.

"I can lock Goldie's view onto my eyes so that normal movement as I walk, or as I turn my head, automatically keeps it with me. That's kind of what you were doing with the arrows wasn't it."

"Yes, except I was moving ahead in time too, fast-forwarding to see where the arrows would go. And then locking that viewpoint. Can you do that?"

"Oh! Is that what you were doing? Well, that's something to try. How far ahead can you go?"

Airlie shrugged. "Not far: it starts to get blurry really quickly when things are changing fast."

Chapter 9

The Quantum Physics session was one Airlie had really been looking forward to: she'd had so many questions. But in fact, it was a major disappointment. Not so much that it was boring, as frustrating — and she had also been distracted by all the fidgeting going on around her.

It had been a series of lectures by half a dozen physicists none of whom could home in on a single theory: it was all 'if' and 'but' and 'alternatively'. Airlie didn't really learn any more than she had got from her reading and googling, though it did seem that most of the physicists found it all just as confusing as she did. The confident ones were the ones with the really wild and woolly theories.

The question-and-answer time had been pretty lack lustre too, until Airlie asked if she could talk about how she understood it. You could have heard a pin drop for a moment, but then she was invited to explain her theory. Her discussion of resonance met nods from most of the older physicists, while the younger ones argued about whether it was just a metaphor or there was a real resonance effect.

Dr Eerdmann was in the room, but until then had only listened. But she picked up on Airlie's discussion on resonance and explained that it fitted well with what they found in EEG — the signals, and the different frequency bands, related to neurons communicating in complexes that developed signature resonances associated with individual sensory-motor events, a phenomenon known as synchrony and binding. She also noted that Airlie had yesterday seemed to synchronize with the resonances in Wendy's brain when they'd gone overtime and redone the BCI experiments with their new EEG electrodes on Airlie, Wendy and Cocoa. Their brains were literally on the same wavelength.

In the end Airlie had managed to achieve resonance with both Wendy and Cocoa without the head-holding.

But right now, she was excited about visiting the collider, and doing an MRI and repeating the experiments with the far more expensive MEG technology. Sooty had not been so pleased about getting into his pet carrier, although calmed down when Airlie projected the route through the woods that they'd be taking.

Wendy was making 'do I really have to go' noises. She couldn't care less about the visit or the brain scans, but was rather overawed that she could now share Cocoa's senses like Kate and Goldie. Except that she couldn't connect on her own and kept asking Airlie to link them.

Sooty obviously wanted to know why the dogs could walk on a lead, but he was in his cage even though he'd been good on his lead that morning. Airlie tapped the connection and tried to explain that it was just because of expectations, but Sooty still couldn't understand — and seemed to be confused by the doggy views and scents that Airlie was sharing.

She confided to Sooty that she was getting over the connection to the dogs too — and much preferred her own senses, enjoying the brisk pine-scented walk down the well-graded track to the collider somewhat more than helter-skelter of glimpsed rabbits or the overwhelming number of poohey scents that Cocoa wanted to investigate.

At least Goldie was so much more disciplined, and she didn't get so much of the smells — or at least hadn't yesterday. *Maybe they had different diets?*

Thinking of Goldie, Airlie was suddenly transported into the other dog's brain. Kate's face filled her vision, and she got a whiff of Kate's scent as she crouched next to him, and a sense of Kate wishing Airlie was there to connect them. *Hi Kate!* She thought.

Airlie saw Kate suddenly jerk up and look around the obstacle course where her group was currently working, then Airlie bumped into Lilly on the track because she wasn't watching where she was going.

Airlie put her hand on Lilly's shoulder for support, and the doggy viewpoint disappeared, returning not to her own vision but blinking through to half a dozen different views of the track that floated around bumping into each other, sometimes coalescing one pair sometimes another.

She held her eyes firmly closed as she tried to take in what she was seeing. Then she felt hairy legs on her hand and a sense of interest and welcome.

That's right! Parker had taken to traveling on Lilly's shoulder when they were out and about, although still preferred to be up her sleeve when they were inside.

Amazingly, Airlie didn't feel anything of the fear she'd had when she'd first been introduced to the huntsman.

"Oh wow!" she said out loud, echoed a moment later by Lilly. "Are you seeing this?" she asked.

"If you mean Parker's kaleidoscope view of the world, I sure am," responded Lilly.

Kaleidoscopic was a good word to describe the way different coloured segments of the world swam into and out of focus, switching from red through orange to green as it focussed on different objects. But in the shadows, blues and violets were in focus and the detail was amazing. Airlie could see insects lurking in the shadowy grooves in the coarse bark of the pine trees. Airlie could almost feel the flight of the unwary fly that circled: it felt like shivers in her arms and legs.

"Don't worry," commented Lilly. "He's fed already. He seems mainly to hunt at dusk and dawn. He was dining on cockroach when I woke up this morning."

Suddenly what they were seeing didn't make sense, and Airlie's stomach whirled so much she thought she was going to be sick. But then she felt okay when she let go of Lilly and reverted to her own vision.

They reached the collider, and it was like seeing the top half of a huge cylinder buried in the dirt, with an igloo-like entrance. But they had to negotiate a security barrier in the wire mesh fence that surrounded it, complete with soldiers and guns. Their guide had both the students and the teachers show their IDs as they passed through the gate one by one. Airlie looked left and right to see the impressive ring segment disappear into the vegetation a few hundred meters away in each direction. The concrete structure had supporting or joining rings every ten metres or so, but ahead of them was an entrance that was all greenish glass and green-painted metal.

Their guide was already explaining. "It's a bit like the London underground or the Paris metro or the New York subway. The Circle line, I guess. Mostly it's underground but here it's above ground, and over there to the right it's partly 'above lake'. The lake is an integral part of the design and plays an essential role in cooling the generators. It also has a role in recreation: canoeing has become quite popular amongst the scientists!"

Chapter 10

Inside the collider ring, they did catch a kind of train but there were no rails: it was kind of a cross between an airline baggage train and an open hospitality cart. The electric motors and rubber wheels were almost silent as they whizzed along past impressive arrays of coils and magnets. Airlie had seen pictures, so much of it was familiar. What was most impressive was the sheer size of it all. In his cat carrier on the seat next to her, Sooty was attentive but unimpressed.

The guide talked for a bit about how it was a multibillion-dollar multinational project trying to resolve fundamental questions in physics by bashing protons and other things together at almost the speed of light. She then explained how they made the charged particles curve and accelerate, and emphasized that the central evacuated tube had to be level because at near the speed of light they couldn't deviate much from the circular path and single plane, and there were some straight parts where the actual collisions happened, where the primary detectors were located behind multiple layers of active and passive electro-magnetic shielding.

That was also where they'd installed the MEG and MRI machines in their own shielded rooms. They were a bit like huge safes, Airlie thought.

She and Sooty were first up for the MEG and would be in the scanners during today's proton injection sequence, and the initial collisions. It was all a bit intimidating.

"Hi! I'm Anne and I'm your medtech for today. You must be Airlie and Sooty." Airlie looked around to see a ginger-haired woman in a green medical gown.

"Before we go into the scanner lab, can you please clean out your pockets and put everything into this tray. And Sooty, we're going to need your collar. Airlie, I see you've got a metal button and zipper on your jeans. You're going to have to them off too, and your bra if you're wearing one. And I need to ask you if either of you have any piercings, or implants or anything else metal on or in your person."

Airlie responded mutely, taking phone and stuff out of her pockets, taking off her jeans and folding them up, running her hands over her chest to demonstrate that she hadn't put on a bra today: she didn't really need one yet. Then she grinned and poked her tongue out at the medtech.

"I'm good! See! No piercings, no braces, no pacemaker, no bra..."

"No nonsense either, by the look of it!" laughed Anne.

"Actually, Nonsense is Yan's dog. You'll have them later on I guess."

Anne scrolled her finger up and down a screen. "Yes, well this session's going to take a few hours, and it looks like she's scheduled for after lunch. The other girl from your school will be in the other lab at the same time: Lilly and Parker it says. We're going to start with an MRI, which gives us the lie of the land so to speak."

Anne steered Airlie over to a bed with a big white donut-shaped headboard.

"Oh! Good idea, make sure I've got my brain in the right place before wondering why things are happening in strange places."

Anne smiled as she got Airlie to lie down in the machine. "This will take a while, forty to fifty minutes maybe, and it's going to be noisy and uncomfortable — but you need to keep still as much as possible. There will be opportunities to breath and change position between scans, and I'll tell you when you can move."

"How are you going to get Sooty to keep still?"

"Actually, we have requested an animal MRI machine, but still normally veterinary subjects are anaesthetized, and we won't want to do that here. So we won't be doing an MRI on Sooty, and for the MEG we'll ask you to hold him and link to him. I gather that leads to a joint conscious state that will be calming for him. It'll be a bit like getting a perm for you both, and it shouldn't be too upsetting for him as it doesn't have to make contact — technically it's designed for *in utero* foetal scans."

"Well, he is my baby!"

Without thinking, Airlie flicked her consciousness over to Sooty in the travel cage, before realizing what she'd done. "Ah! For this MRI, should I be linked with Sooty or not."

Anne nodded her head to the mirror opposite the machines. "Behind that you've got some boffins who will instruct you when to do what. But for starters I'd say we'll want a reference scan of just you, without any link to anyone or anything else."

"Hi Airlie! It's Natalie Eerdmann here, can you hear me?"

"Hi Dr Eerdmann! You're coming through loud and clear."

"Great! Prof. Freund is here too. You look as if you might have connected to Sooty just then. I understand that you wanted to check in on him and give him some support. But it would be good if you can unlink for the first twenty minutes, and then we'll get you to connect and we'll see what happens when you try to shift perspectives. We'll be trying to home in on which parts of the brain are involved in that."

That first twenty minutes seemed to take forever, and Airlie tried to concentrate on the sound of the MRI machine, and started to track where it was in its scan — but she felt her vision track the sound and stopped that to avoid disrupting the initial scan. So she just concentrated on what she heard and what she felt, physically, trying to understand exactly what it was that was so unpleasant and uncomfortable when all it was *was* that she wasn't allowed to move. Despite not being linked, Airlie's discomfort seemed to communicate itself to Sooty.

"Are you sure you weren't connected to Sooty?" Dr Eerdmann asked.

"No, I consciously avoided connecting, although I could hear him getting restless."

Then Airlie heard Prof. Freund's voice in the background. "I think Natalie, that for the next subject we'll have the animal kept in the anteroom."

There was a break for half a minute and then Dr Eerdmann was back. "We're just about to start on Wendy in the other room, and have had her take Cocoa out and give

84

him a bone to keep him amused while we do her preliminary scan: he really didn't like the whine of the MRI machine. And now that your initial scan is finished, we'll take turns in giving you mental tasks to do. We'll be alternating between you and Wendy, and down the track will also ask you to try to link with her and Cocoa."

With some interesting things to do, and the link to Sooty, the next half hour went quickly, and the tasks involving linking to Sooty and shifting her perspective were now second nature. Finally, it was time to connect to Wendy and Cocoa, and that was something she'd only done a couple of times before. And at first it had involved actual physical contact. Although she *had* managed to connect to Kate on the way over.

Airlie closed her eyes again and tracked her perspective around to the other side of the observation room and found Wendy, with Cocoa lying on the floor next to her MRI bed.

"OK, I have Wendy and Cocoa in view now, and am trying to connect to Cocoa."

Suddenly her view washed out and it took Airlie a moment to make sense of what she was seeing. She had a view of the top of the observation mirror and much of the ceiling — and something that she eventually realized was Wendy's hand gripping the edge of the bed.

She tried to look at Wendy, and Cocoa stirred, getting to his feet and sniffing around inquisitively before looking across at Wendy, who was lying on her back facing the ceiling, but Airlie could just make out that she had her eyes closed — and seemed to be grimacing.

"OK, trying to link in Wendy now."

Cocoa moved forward and pushed his nose into Wendy's hand — and Airlie got a strong whiff of her earthy scent. Wendy recognized Cocoa and moved her hand onto his head — and Airlie could feel her scratching her/him behind the ears.

Then Wendy spoke and somehow it was like hearing it and thinking it at the same time, except her voice sounded somewhat tinny. "I'm seeing me! I'm seeing through Cocoa's eyes!"

"Look at Cocoa, Wendy," Airlie suggested. "But don't move your head," she added belatedly.

Wendy clearly 'heard' her, and fortunately just opened her eyes and swivelled them towards Cocoa. Suddenly Airlie switched to her viewpoint, and then raised her viewpoint above the bed to see both Wendy and Cocoa.

"Ah! I think I muffed it — I'm just getting my remote perspective now."

"But I'm seeing it," said Wendy. "I can see myself on the bed, and Cocoa next to me."

This was getting confusing, and suddenly Airlie felt exhausted. And that was just the first hour or so. Yet to come was three hours of MEG.

Dr Eerdmann's microphone snapped on again and her voice sounded around both rooms, tinged with awe and suppressed excitement. "That was great Airlie, but I can see you getting tired. We'll take a break before the MEG."

In the background, Prof. Freund was muttering incredulously — something about synchronization in the precuneus. Airlie flipped her viewpoint into the observation room to see what he was so excited about.

Airlie's stomach was growling by the time they finished the MEG — despite having had a drink break at a couple of points. Sooty was also starting to get irritated — but they had both food and water for him.

After getting dressed, Airlie found Dr Eerdmann waiting at the door of the lab for her. "Ready for some lunch?"

Sooty was back in his carrier on the train with some of Dr Eerdmann's animal behaviour people, as they headed back to the igloo entrance and its cafeteria. Airlie connected to him and saw his claustrophobic point of view for a moment before flipping to hers. Hopefully experiencing what she was seeing and sensing would relieve the stress.

"That was another thought-provoking session," Dr Eerdmann said. "I don't know that there's much to inform any of the quantum theories, but we could certainly see resonances in the MEG, as well as corresponding areas showing activity in the functional MRI. My team will try and integrate it all together onto a single brain map per activity, including topological fitting of Sooty's scans with yours."

"Can I see my brain maps when they're done?" Airlie asked.

"Of course!" Dr Eerdmann responded. She paused for a moment before continuing thoughtfully. "Next time, we might try to encourage more vocalization, talking your way through exactly what you're thinking and doing and feeling and sensing. This will add some additional elements of speech, language and sensorimotor activity, but with the first scan as a reference we can cancel out those confusion variables and we'll get better insights into what's going on in that weird and wonderful head of yours."

"I tried to tell you what I was doing, just before trying it."

"Yes, that's good and very important for understanding what's going on. But we need to tell you when to do so, as usually it's important for you not to engage in any uncalled for motor activity."

Chapter 11

Running again! But this time Airlie wasn't feeling quite so puffed, and right now she was jogging along in the second last group, with Sooty running ahead of her or behind her or around her. It was like they were connected by a rubber band and Airlie could always sense where she was, and sensed that Sooty was keeping close tabs on where she was — and she was also getting all sorts of scents from her too. But they smelt quite different from the doggy senses she got from Goldie and Cocoa.

'Woof!' Thinking of Goldie had triggered a brief connection and Goldie had noticed. Kate was doing surprisingly well, keeping up with her despite using Goldie's eyes. Most of her cabin and Kate's was ahead of them but Lilly and a couple of others were lagging still further behind.

Airlie felt herself pulled into Goldie/Kate's mind and out of her own perspective. 'Wish you could connect to me. But don't get too close!' Kate said in her head. 'It's too hard for me to recognize any hazards coming up if we're right behind people.'

'Wow! This solves the problem of being too puffed to talk,' Airlie responded in kind, stumbling as she sought to adjust to an intermediate perspective that showed more of the ground but was still close to Kate's viewpoint.

'What! You can hear me?' Kate thought.

Suddenly the group ahead of them vanished from view and they could see the empty track ahead.

'What did you do?' asked Kate.

'Dunno,' Airlie responded. 'Just tried to get a viewpoint as if the others weren't there.'

Airlie shifted perspective again and the girls ahead of them reappeared. Then she made them disappear again. 'I don't know what's happening...'

'Well, it certainly feels safer to me having a clear view ahead on the track. I'm not used to moving this fast, or even seeing with Goldie's eyes. Things I see ahead just arrive too quickly, 'cause it takes a while for me to figure out what we're seeing.'

'Goldie seems to have adapted well. Though this probably contradicts her training.'

'Her guide-dog training, definitely! But we've been practicing running obstacle courses in our animal handling groups here at camp.'

Whoosh! Thwunk! An arrow quivered in a tree just ahead of them. "Down!" Airlie shouted, pulling Kate to the ground. "Someone's shooting at us!"

The green fletching told Airlie it was one of the camp arrows, but the archery equipment wasn't allowed to be taken off the range. "Stop!" Airlie tried calling out to whoever was out there with bows and arrows. "There's people on the path here!"

There was no sign of Airlie's or Kate's roommates, but Airlie reached out with her senses, looking for the rogue

90

archers. There were eight boys and the archery trainer. *What's going on?*

"Mr Fletcher! What are you doing out here shooting near the jogging track! There are two groups of girls here, out for our usual morning run!"

Mr Fletcher jumped and looked around as if he thought she was right next to him, twisting his head back and forth with a look of astonishment on his face. He held up his hand commandingly. "Stop! No shooting! There are people around..." He continued to look around in a confused way.

"Who's there? This is a hunting preserve, and the eastern tracks are all signposted with warnings."

Now it was Airlie's turn to be confused. Airlie cast her senses around for their roommates and found Lilly's group just ahead of them — and others way ahead of them. "Lilly," Airlie called out. "Be careful there are people shooting arrows around here."

Airlie pointed at the tree, but to her surprise she couldn't see the arrow at first, and then suddenly there was the arrow, and she was on her own.

In a panic, she wrenched the arrow from the tree, then sought out her friends again. They appeared in a blink of the eye, screaming in shock. "Where were you? Lilly called out. "You just disappeared on us. And where did that arrow come from?"

Airlie didn't answer. She felt so tired, exhausted... A black tunnel seemed to rush at her and she clasped at Kate's arm. She felt other hands grasp at her as the darkness became all encompassing... And then nothing...

Chapter 12

Airlie woke to a soft chorus of unfamiliar sounds: beeps and gurgles and heavy breathing. She opened her eyes to muted light. Turning her head slightly, she recognized that she was in a clinic. The walls and mirror looked familiar: she was at the collider.

There was an unfamiliar man sitting on a chair in the corner, plumpish, his mouth slightly open as he breathed, paper rustling as he turned a page. Then his eyes met hers and he stood and introduced himself.

"Hello Airlie! I'm Denis, Denis McLaughlin. How are you feeling?" He took a couple of steps closer to the bed.

"Fine, I guess. Are you a doctor?"

"No, I'm a chaplain. The police chaplain for Minor Affairs. Your camp application form had your religion as Baptist. I'm actually Uniting though."

"Okay... Well, I won't hold that against you."

The chaplain shuffled awkwardly, and Airlie started to sit up. He took a step forward, holding up his hand. "Don't do that! You might pull out your drip or your wires. There's a nurse who's been looking in on you every half-hour. She should be here shortly. Maybe it would be easier if I sat again."

Airlie shrugged as best she could, and tracked the guy as he stepped back and eased himself down into his chair.

"So what do you make of all this psychic powers stuff?" Airlie asked. "How does it fit in with God and all that? You do know why we're here don't you?"

"Yes, I know about the so-called quantum talents. I've had quite a few counselling sessions with kids and parents who ahh..."

"Who think they're going crazy?" Airlie supplied.

"Well sometimes... Or in some case they are concerned that it's the devil at work... Or sometimes they ask whether it's a gift from God... Or some people don't know what to think and just want to talk... I remind them of Jesus' parable of the talents and suggest they do look at it as a gift from God: he works everything for his purposes. This means the real question is what God means you to achieve with it."

Airlie considered that for a moment, then put aside the question of whether there was some divine purpose behind her gift, focussing on the privacy aspect. "I'll bet it's hard to keep a lid on it with people talking to counsellors and psychologists, or ministers or social workers... I mean, how did Minor Affairs even get to know about it, let alone be running the show?"

"Your case was one of the first, Airlie. And there were others that came to our attention in similar ways, and several came via the social workers. Then some people approached university psychology departments, or got referrals to psychologists or psychiatrists. And, of course, Minor Affairs did the same. We set up a special referral centre, and medical practices and school and church counsellors all now know what to look out for, although we haven't publicized the quantum or collider connections, or even that they are real gifts. For most health professionals, I think it just looks like another aspect of the current mental health epidemic."

"So how does it relate to God, miracles and all that? Does it make you question your beliefs?"

"No more than anything else that science and technology have challenged us with over the course of my lifetime." The chaplain spread his hands out and grimaced.

"So many scientists think they know everything, or at least think that science can already explain pretty much everything. And the non-scientists and pseudoscientists are even worse in this respect, as real scientists know you can't ever prove a theory. Really things like biology and the theory of evolution, and physics and the theory of the big bang, are just edifices of assumptions and circular arguments that are not really worthy of the label 'theory'. There are many tiny bits that can be explained, sometimes even big bits, but the overwhelming answer to the really big questions is either 'we can't know for certain' or 'we don't know at all'. It's good to see God throw the scientists a curve ball occasionally!"

"But there's also ideas about plausibility and parsimony and so on." Airlie remembered reading stuff about the scientific method and Occam's razor, and KISS or Keep It Simple Stupid. But before she could get her head around her next question, Anne appeared at the door.

The ginger-haired medtech walked briskly over to the bed. "So Airlie, you're awake! You gave us all a scare, not to mention setting tongues wagging. How are you feeling?"

While they chatted, Anne busied herself disconnecting Airlie from the array of monitoring gear. When she was done, Anne help Airlie sit up and looked her straight in the eyes. "There's a stack of people out there waiting to talk to you. There are your friends" — she jerked her thumb one way — "and there's the boffins" — she pointed a finger the other way.

"I think I'd better let my friends know I'm alright first, and then we can go and see your boffins together!"

Anne started to remonstrate. "They won't like..."

But Airlie was already seeking out Sooty, and cut her off. "If they want to talk to me, they can talk to the lot of us. We're in this together, and if there's any dangers to worry about then we all need to know about them."

Airlie couldn't resist taking a virtual peek to see just which friends it was who were waiting for her... and which boffins...

Anne stepped close to the mirror and Airlie could just make out her soft words. "Natalie, she's fine. But she is a bit sensitive about meeting with all these heavies, and insists on having her friends with her. She's right you know: they are all involved. They all need to know what's going on. Whatever happened, it could happen to them too. It did happen to Kate."

Airlie and Kate followed Anne up the circular corridor with Goldie, followed by Yan and Lilly, and Wendy and Cocoa. Sooty shot ahead of Anne and then sat down to wait at an open doorway, peeking tentatively inside. Natalie

Eerdmann popped out, crouching to pet Sooty's head as she looked back towards Airlie and her friends. "Good to see you back in the land of the living, Airlie," she called out. "We were worried."

Natalie glanced back into the room for a moment, turning back as Airlie and Kate reached them. "Hi Airlie! Yes, you are welcome to bring your friends in, although there might be a shortage of seats. But you and Kate can sit here."

Natalie stepped through the doorway and ushered them to some seats just inside. She was right. There weren't many seats and some of the scientists were leaning against benches while Mr Fletcher just stood there, arms crossed and a morose look on his face, his back to the observation window. Inspector Humble stood next to him wearing a friendly smile and looking much more relaxed.

The lab was clearly designed to accommodate 6 scientists (based on the number of workstations and lab stools), not 16 people plus two dogs and a cat. Prof. Freund looked rather peeved about it all.

Anne moved into the doorway and addressed the room. "Sorry everyone. We did ask them to build us a conference room, but this as a big as we can do — unless you want to meet in the cafeteria. We do use that for news conferences, you know."

"This will do fine, Anne" responded Natalie. "I think you all know Airlie, and perhaps Kate. Kate is the blind girl who was involved in the incident — and has the grazes to prove it. She felt the breeze as the arrow whipped past her too. And these are Yan, Lilly and Wendy who are bunkmates that she's been working closely with — and they were just ahead of or behind Airlie and Kate on the track when the incident happened, when they just disappeared."

"Yes, we've all heard Lilly and Kate's stories about me and my archery group and the arrow," said Mr Fletcher in a rather irritated tone. "Except we weren't there, and Airlie didn't talk to me. We did consider using that area as a hunting range, but that was vetoed by the committee as too dangerous — and the archery range is on the other side of the campsite, and that's where I was."

"The vote?" Airlie asked. "The vote about the hunting range? Was it close?"

"'Close,' she asks. Yes, it was close! There was only a single vote in it. But now all we have is fixed target shooting."

"Good question, Airlie." The voice came from the back of the room, from one of the physics profs. "We've been thinking along the same lines, or parallel lines you might say..."

Inspector Humble interrupted. "I think at this point we need to allow Airlie to give her account of what happened. She and her friends have had a very trying day. You'll have the opportunity to talk about your theories later."

It didn't take Airlie long to talk her way through the incident, although she was distracted by Mr Fletcher's fuming face. He seemed to be getting more and more incensed. So she turned to address him. "I know it wasn't you, Mr Fletcher. It was another you, another Mr Fletcher. I think I can explore possible worlds almost as easily as actual perspectives on this world. That would also explain what happened in an earlier case too... I think that the more likely a possibility is, the more sharply I can see that actual alternate universe, or in this case even slip sideways into it…and even take someone with me, or bring something back…"

"See! It's not some esoteric theory you need a PhD to understand." The physicist at the back of the room was gesticulating excitedly. "Even an eleven-year-old can see that this is what's happening. And yes, highly probable events can act as attractors. And with 'just one vote in it' that archery range would be at a highly probable nexus of possible worlds."

"But how did she get there…"

"And why did she faint…"

"Dimensional transfer would take a huge amount of energy…"

"Well, whatever it is, she should only try it again under controlled conditions. We need to keep her here at the lab while we work out what happened."

Fortunately, calmer and more ethical heads prevailed, and Airlie and her friends were able to enjoy exploring their new gifts together for the rest of the camp.

Kate, Yan, Wendy and Lilly had all managed to persuade their parents to let them transfer into the Opportunity Classes at the Maths and Science school.

For the first time in their lives, they couldn't wait for school to start back! It was going to be fantastic.

PART THREE

GONE

Chapter 13

Home awkward home! There was nothing sweet about it: Peter was being a pain as usual (she was now an officially certified weirdo); Dad was after details about the camp that she didn't want to give (she hadn't mentioned anything about the arrow incident or them wanting to keep her at the collider as a lab rat); and Mum had a never-ending list of holiday chores she wanted done before school went back (her new school was part of that as she needed a school uniform, a sports uniform, and specific supplies for the opportunity class).

At least Peter knew that the camp had something to do with her mysterious detective skills, and him calling her weird was nothing new. But her friends, her old friends that weren't at camp and weren't coming to the new school… They didn't seem to want anything to do with her or Yan: they always had plans, the cliques were tighter, and there were whispers.

Lilly seemed to have it a bit easier, because she hadn't been accepted for the OC class and got to do some things with friends from her wind ensemble and dance group — until they noticed Parker. Then the questions started:

'He adopted you?'

'The camp allowed you to keep it?'

'Since when are there police spiders?'

But the same day, Lilly got a letter of offer from the Science and Mathematics school, explaining that she'd been waitlisted and was being offered a place. A few minutes later, Lilly's mum was on the phone asking Airlie and Yan round for dinner so that they could talk about the offer.

"It all sounds a bit fishy to me," Mrs Fredricks said, as she served out the salad. "Lilly's never been particularly interested in Science, and she's always struggled with Maths. I don't understand why they'd make her the offer. I mean, she really just applied because you two did. It's got something to do with that camp hasn't it, and that spider?"

Airlie and Yan looked at each other, and then at Lilly. "Yes it has, Mrs Fredricks," Airlie responded. "Do you remember that confidentiality agreement the police had you sign?"

Mrs Fredricks nodded. "Yes, I've got it here." She shuffled out some papers from the back of a pile of brochures and about the school offer. "It was very comprehensive, and I was surprised about some aspects of it. Not so much the paragraphs about police procedure and training methods, but the mention of new scientific discoveries and experimental technologies. And the list of weird sciences which, come to think of it, seem suspiciously similar to those listed for the new school."

She grimaced at the two-page confidentiality document.

"It's weirder than you think, Mrs Fredricks, and we can only talk to you about it because you signed that agreement. And yes, the offers to the OC class are related. And the spider may well have been the deciding factor in Lilly getting an offer."

Parker chose that moment to pop his head out from Lilly's collar and stared at her mum, who stared right back. She looked from Lilly and the spider to her husband, and then back to Airlie and Yan.

"The camp director, Inspector Humble, said we had to use discretion," Yan explained. "We can talk about stuff to anyone that signed the letter. Which means any of the parents, but not brothers or sisters or other relatives."

"It's actually a bit like science fiction," Airlie said. "You might find it hard to believe. Which is I guess why Lilly wanted us here. We might have to show you. Although the most impressive demonstration would be…"

Suddenly Airlie went into shock.

It was Kate. Something was happening to her.

Chapter 14

"Can I make a phone call? I need to call Inspector Humble."

Airlie grabbed the police letterhead that Lilly's mum had unearthed. She tried to control her breathing and her panic before she dialled, and as she listened to the ring tone.

"Minor Affairs! How can I direct your call?"

"Inspector Humble please!"

"It's after 5! Can it wait till tomorrow? Or can someone else help?"

"Sergeant Sanford, or Sergeant Marks maybe."

"No, they are not available at present. Can I take your number and leave a message to call you?"

"No! I've been strictly instructed not to talk to anyone else about it, and it's urgent: a crime in progress. Please put me through to Inspector Humble now, wherever he is. Tell him it's Airlie Sanderson. He'll talk to me."

"He would have my head if I did that..."

"He'll have your head if you don't." Airlie homes in on the receptionist and virtually glares at her. She doesn't seem to notice.

Airlie is vaguely aware of the policewoman saying something, but her focus is on the reception desk and the office behind it. She casts her sight down a corridor, peeking behind each closed door. There's an open area at the end but inside the last door on the right she finds Humble and Marks. They're interviewing someone.

Airlie tries to reach Humble's mind, then Marks's, then Humble's again.

"Look! I know Humble and Marks are there in an interview," she says out loud while trying to convey the same thought to Humble. "They can interrupt it..." *Interrupt it...*

Airlie continues into the open area where there are about eight work areas, but only three are occupied. Is that El? She spins around her perspective and tries to get through to her. "Sergeant Sanford is at her desk. Just call her!"

Airlie's vaguely aware that the woman at the reception desk is getting annoyed, but pulls her attention back to Humble and Marks. She tries to project her face into their minds.

Suddenly Sergeant Marks taps at his wrist with two fingers, and Inspector Humble declares a break and stops the recording. Airlie loses track of them momentarily as they leave the room.

Then Humble lifts a phone, and a moment later she hears a phone ring. She hears the receptionist answer. She hears both sides of the conversation.

"Has anything come up that I need to deal with?" asks Humble.

"There's a young girl called Airlie on the line, something about a crime... but she'll talk only to you."

"Put her through to my office! I'll be there in a jiffy." Humble slams down his receiver and just about runs down the corridor.

I must have got through a bit, Airlie realizes.

Airlie tracks Humble back to his office where he leans over his desk and grabs a ringing phone. "Hello Airlie?" he asks as Sanford and Marks appear in his doorway, and Marks knocks on the open door. "Hold on, putting you on speaker. Marks and Sanford have just appeared." He beckons them in and signals Sanford to close the door.

"Kate and Goldie have been kidnapped," Airlie yells.

Chapter 15

While the police were on their way, Airlie checked her address book and homed in on Kate's house. All seemed quiet.

She connected to Kate and Goldie, but all was dark although there was a strange oily smell in the air, and the sound of a quiet motor and tires on the road, and the feel of something tied around her head. Then they were pressed together as the car took a corner. There was a squeal of tires as another car followed. It sounded like at least two cars in convoy.

She sent her sight to Kate's home again and then pulled up into the air, looking for a convoy of fast driving vehicles — and found one.

Two police cars with flashing lights were heading towards Kate's place. Then she heard sirens as two cars pulled up with a screech outside Lilly's house.

Chapter 16

Airlie's worries gave way to a hint of excitement as Lieutenant Sanford pulled away from Lilly's in an unmarked police car with a flashing light on the roof, and a tinge of disappointment as El didn't use her siren. The marked police car in front raced ahead though, clearing the way with occasional bursts of siren at the busy intersections.

They stopped next to a couple of police cars in an unfamiliar neighbourhood. The inspector hopped out and went over to them, while El explained that this was where Kate had been for her guitar lesson and they were canvassing the neighbours to see if they'd seen anything. The inspector walked Kate's route home, with El keeping pace in the car. They'd already identified the kidnap location from Airlie's description. The kidnappers' vehicles had evidently been parked near a corner ready to swoop as soon as Kate turned out of sight of her music teacher's home.

Next thing she knew, they were pulling onto the grass alongside two police cars outside Kate's house, which Airlie also recognized from her farsight view.

A uniformed policewoman at the front door nodded at Inspector Humble and Sergeant Sanford, her eyes scanning Airlie neutrally. In the hallway, another officer showed them into a living room where for a moment it seemed Airlie was seeing two copies of Kate. Their eyes turned toward them as they came in. They clearly weren't blind, but they had the same brown hair and eyes and features as Kate. Except that her mum's eyes were red and raw, and the boy's eyes glistened as he hugged his mum and tried to be brave for her.

One of the two cops in the room came over to brief the inspector. Kate should have been home an hour ago, around the time when Airlie had the flash of fear and darkness from her. Kate wasn't answering her phone.

But really the only evidence that she'd been kidnapped was Airlie's 'vision', which so far had been treated as if it were an anonymous tip by an eyewitness. Airlie's heart leapt into her throat as she realized that all of this was hanging on her.

"Good evening, Mrs Leskie." I'm Inspector Humble and this is Sergeant Sanford. "I'm wondering if we can have a moment alone with you. Perhaps the officers can take your son to the kitchen to organize some refreshments. And I'd like to introduce you to Airlie Sanderson who's a friend of Kate's, and our witness."

The boy perked up momentarily. "You're Airlie? Kate's told me so much about you. You're the one that taught her to see properly. Can you tell us more about what happened?"

Mrs Leskie got to her feet and pulled Airlie into a hug. "Kate couldn't stop talking about you. I know you'll be able to help us find her." She turned to the inspector and continued. "Whether it's things you think need to be kept confidential or things that you think will upset him, I think Tim needs to stay here with us. He deserves to hear it all."

"He's got the gift," Airlie added. "I can sense something."

Inspector Humble looked at them both for a moment, and then at the two police officers. "Fair enough! But I still think we need to organize that cuppa. Do you mind if we use your kitchen? El can you take people's orders and pass them on to the guys outside?"

As she stood there awkwardly, the everyday routine of drink orders being taken gave Airlie time to shut her eyes briefly and focus in on Kate and Goldie, but her thoughts wandered back to Tim. Kate had mentioned a brother in passing, but Tim might be a twin, or at most a year older or younger. She opened her eyes to find him staring at her.

As their eyes met, Airlie felt a twinge of mental contact. Evidently Tim did too. He invited her to have a seat on the lounge next to him, and then whispered. "Kate tried to teach me to connect to Goldie too, but it didn't seem to work. Except that sometimes I felt there was almost a connection, just like with you just now. Can you help connect me to Kate?"

Inspector Humble cleared his throat and sounded almost apologetic. "It seems that our ploy of fitting Kate with a dummy occipital implant transceiver wasn't effective. And obviously within the family, it couldn't really work. So Tim, I gather Kate's shared everything with you."

Airlie hadn't known about this, and the inspector quickly explained that Kate didn't actually have an implant, but they'd provided her with a transceiver to wear to explain her new ability to see. It was like a pair of glasses with an integrated headband that went round the back of her head.

While the inspector quizzed Tim about what Kate had told him, Airlie connected to Kate and Goldie and tried to sense this interface headset. It was disconcerting to see only a hint of light through the dog's blindfold, and that seemed to make it harder to trace back, but every time she tried it was a bit easier. She traced back quickly to the point where a hood was put over Goldie's head, but rather than following forward as they were bundled into the van, she tried to get into Kate's head.

It felt much the same, but why would they put a hood over a blind girl's head? She could feel it bump against her headset glasses, could feel them push down on her ears and nose. She could feel something bind her jaw closed and force the band of contacts into the back and sides of her head. Why didn't they take the transceiver off? If they knew about the expensive implant and transceiver technology, surely they'd take it. The transceiver was the real deal, even though Kate didn't actually have an implant.

Why couldn't she communicate back and forth with Kate as happened spontaneously on the track at camp, just before that arrow incident? They'd never been able to reproduce that.

Airlie reviewed the incident from Goldie's perspective too. Was that a prick she felt just before the hood went on? Did Goldie somehow feel more sluggish than usual? It seemed like it was hard for her to walk as she was dragged into the van. But mentally, perceptually, it all seemed pretty normal — as far as she could tell with the hood on, and her muzzle taped.

She traced back beyond the moment the hood was put on to the glimpse of black vehicles pulling up a moment before, and then before that to their everyday walk down the street.

Airlie shifted Goldie's vision as far as she could and again saw the three vehicles, black vehicles, two black cars bracketing some kind of van, indistinct men leaping from the cars before they'd even come to a full stop. She saw two men grab at her and struggle for a moment before one got the hood on and the other bound it around with tape. She was left with a kind of hospital smell lingering in her nose. So she had been injected with something.

It was only with great effort that Airlie stopped herself following along with Goldie as they were bundled into the van. She tried to anchor her vision there as the convoy moved off. Maybe it was the doggy vision, but she still couldn't make out any number plates.

She thought about how El had taken her along Kate's route home from her guitar lesson, and she'd identified where the kidnapping had taken place. And now that she'd been there, maybe she and Sooty could explore the possibilities of the area the way they had with their dog case. But at the moment she couldn't manage anything more.

Suddenly Airlie was aware of her name being mentioned and pulled the inspector's last few sentences out of her quantum enhanced memory.

"I should also clarify that while the police officers in this room are part of Minor Affairs, the two in the corridor are not. Also, the Kidnapping and Extortion Unit have not been read in as yet, and it is also important to understand that the law does not yet recognize a role for quantum gifts, or witnesses such as Airlie."

"What does that mean?" sobbed Mrs Leskie. "Are you saying you can't look for Kate?"

"Minor Cases can look for Kate, and we can draw resources from KEU for the first 72 hours after the disappearance of a minor. But there are legal limitations on what we can do based on information that comes from the new gifts without being independently validated."

Then Airlie was asked to go through what she'd managed to see through Goldie's eyes.

As she explained it, she closed her eyes and experienced it all again. But this time she felt that mental contact from Tim spike through and get an answer from Goldie. She grabbed hold of the fleeting impressions and connected them.

Tim gasped. "Wow," he said. "It's like a spy movie. The three black vehicles follow Kate around the corner into Binder St and then, with military precision, the doors open and three operatives in black suits are out in a trice. And moments later, have bundled Kate and me... I mean Goldie... into the van."

"What's going on here?" asked Sergeant Sanford. "How is this possible?"

"Oh! This is the easy bit," Airlie responded airily. "Tim has a bit of a connection to Goldie as well and asked me to connect him. Then when I was connected to Goldie I felt his probe and Goldie's response, and I just held the connection together till it stabilized. Just like when I first connected to Kate and Goldie at camp."

"And what is the hard bit?" Inspector Humble asked.

"The hard bit is understanding how Kate and I can get perspectives that Goldie has never seen. Though as you know, the quantum neuroscientists at camp had some ideas about that."

"Actually," Sergeant Sanford put in. "We haven't gone through all the theories that the scientists have come up with. There are far too many of them, and most of them are far too flakey to take seriously. But if this is going to be accepted as evidence, maybe we do need some understanding of this point."

"Well, this is not so much a theory as an association of ideas. When someone said you can't see things you can't look at, Professor Eerdmann reminded us that almost all vision is like this. I mean, you can only properly see what is in a tiny region called the fovea. What we really see is kind of a combination of memory and low resolution info, with the eye jumping around to fill in the detail. So what we think we see is mostly an illusion. It's like virtual reality."

"Thanks Airlie, that does ring some bells," the inspector commented thoughtfully. "But it's all rather vague. I couldn't take it to a judge, and there's no expert witness who would stand up in court." The inspector sounded rather dubious and out of sorts, but visibly perked up as the smell of brewing coffee hit the air.

"I understand. As I said, it's not really a theory yet." Airlie paused for a moment before continuing. "The quantum and dimensional side of my gifts are, I think, quite distinct. The quantum coupling directly involves quantum-paired brains. But the dimensional twisting and jumping doesn't seem to involve multiple brains: the quantum thing is maybe a kind of catalyst. Still somehow Kate's combined the two and is seeing from different perspectives using dog vision. I guess it's because it is the only model for vision that her brain can construct. On the other hand, she's got the advantage over me that almost her entire visual cortex is available for this new kind of sight. She should be able to..."

"How's this help us find Kate?" Mrs Leskie interjected with some annoyance.

"I'm sorry, Mrs Leskie. We are already doing all we can. We've got police cars and helicopters scouring the vicinity for those vehicles, and we've got people looking at satellite imagery as well. Airlie's information has given us a much better start than we'd normally have, as well as launching the search far earlier than it would have been otherwise. So, at this point, exploring what Airlie can do and integrating that with what you can contribute as family... That's the best thing we can do."

"Actually, it's not just a matter of what I can do," added Airlie, "it's a matter of what Goldie and Kate and Tim and I can do. As I was just saying, Kate has much more brain real estate to allocate to this, because what would normally be doing normal vision can be used for quantum dimensional vision. Also, I'm sure that Kate and Goldie are aware of me connecting to them, I can sense them react, even though Kate can't connect through my ears and eyes. But perhaps she can connect through Tim, since being in the same household he should have quantum entanglement with both of them."

Mrs Leskie drew in her breath sharply and flicked her eyes from Airlie to Tim and back.

At that moment, there was a knock on the door, followed by a flurry of tea, coffee and biscuit arrangements.

120

"Mrs Leskie," Airlie asked hesitantly after a while. "Could Tim come over to my place? Having Sooty would help, but not here. I think it needs to be in his familiar environment. We have a guest room. Actually, you both could come and stay with us. I'm sure Mum and Dad wouldn't mind in the circumstances."

"What about if there's a ransom call?"

Inspector Humble answered that. "I don't really think there will be a ransom call in this case. The kidnapping most likely relates to either the quantum gifts or the implant technology. But in any case, you can take your mobile and we can forward the landline to it. It won't affect our ability to trace any calls, and it probably isn't a good idea for you to be alone. It also makes it easier for us to keep an eye on both Airlie and Tim — and Sooty for that matter. If you like, I can ring Airlie's parents to make the arrangements. I've been keeping them in the loop, and they've said they are happy to help in any way they can."

In the backseat of El's unmarked police car, Tim quizzed Airlie. "How is me linking to Kate going to help? You can already link to her."

"Two reasons," Airlie replied. "First, there's a good chance your connection via Goldie can go both ways. Second, if you can transmit visual information, you'll give her a chance to learn human visual brain patterns and open up the possibility of two-way communication, although this will likely take a couple of days."

"How come it will take a few days?"

"There have been experiments, inverting normal vision with lenses or prisms, or restricting the range of movement with special collars. The initial transformation can take the best part of a week. Kate said it took about five days for her to get used to seeing through Goldie's eyes and fully make sense of it. But subsequent adjustments are always faster. It only took a couple of days for Kate to become fully comfortable with an elevated perspective. So reverting dog two-colour vision back to human three-color vision should be quicker — and hopefully we can teach her to read too."

Airlie leant forward to talk to Sergeant Sanford. "El, can you get us some alphabet books and early picture book readers... As many as possible, like a dozen, with pictures of different things. And also some Braille to English training charts."

"I saw some Braille/English overlay signage like this at the Olympics a few years ago. Is that what you want?" El looked at her in the mirror. "I think I can see where you're heading here... Sounds like something worthwhile to explore. I'll get someone on to it."

Chapter 17

Airlie reached out to Sooty as they pulled up at the house, and Sooty met them at the door. She wondered for the umpteenth time why she couldn't see through Sooty's eyes, but could easily track to where he was, or around where he was. Or where she was. But when they were together, she seemed to be able to move her sight more freely. Or when she was with Goldie or Cocoa for that matter. But since camp, it was increasingly difficult to connect to them.

"Tim, are you still connected to Kate and Goldie?" she asked as they headed up the path to the house.

"No, I lost the connection when we got into the explanations."

"Okay, well Sooty's waiting at the door with Mum and Dad. We'll say a quick hello and go upstairs and get connected again as soon as possible. Try to keep the connection going and transmit your visual and sensory impressions to her. Concentrate on what you can see, on the different colours, on what you can hear, on the different tones."

The front door opened as she was speaking, and Sooty rubbed across her legs as she went in. Peter appeared behind Mum and Dad, and Airlie introduced everyone to Tim.

"Sorry, there's no time to waste. We'll be in my room connecting with Kate. I'll leave Inspector Humble to introduce everyone and explain everything."

Sooty bounded up ahead, and Airlie had Tim follow him up the stairs ahead of her. Sooty jumped up onto Airlie's bed and she and Tim sat on each side of him, but then the cat moved into her lap and after a few turns settled down for a pat.

"Move closer to me and gently pat his back while I caress his head and chuck him under the chin. Try to maintain contact with Sooty at all times, even if you're just resting your hand on him. When I connect to Kate, try to probe me as you did before, but try to sense Kate and Goldie directly and reach out to them directly."

Airlie found it easy to connect to Kate and Goldie and sensed that they were trying to make contact with her. She felt the probe from Tim and connected him to Goldie again. Then she tried to make contact with Kate, and got a sense of her. It seemed she wasn't in the car anymore. There wasn't that sense of motion, and there seemed to be more space around her. But was Tim sensing all this?

Airlie tried to pull back her senses and see the room, but although things seemed to shift they remained dark. Suddenly she flipped back into Goldie's perspective. She tried to rewind to the point when the car stopped, and then listened as doors slammed. Then she heard muffled growls and grunts.

Now she pulled back till she was conscious of her connection and yes, the connection with Tim was still there. She drew on Sooty and tried to strengthen it. She tried to connect through to Tim. What was he sensing? What was he seeing?

He was looking at her. Suddenly she could see herself and her hand on Sooty's head. Her light brown hair had lightened to a golden blond during the summer, and her hazel eyes seemed to have a tinge of gold too. And her pink top was pink rather than the murky yellowy colour she saw through doggy eyes.

Kate's link suddenly jerked. Maybe she was seeing this. Would she recognize her?

Airlie reached out and felt around on her bedside chest of drawers. Could she find a mirror? She pulled open the drawer and scrabbled around trying to find the old compact she kept in there. Tim's view followed her. She tried pulling it around to her perspective, like she'd taught Kate to do. She could see the top of the chest but not into the drawer. She released her touch on Sooty as she leant further across and found the compact. Tim's vision persisted. She/he could see the compact. She flipped it open and adjusted it, so Tim's face was visible.

Kate's link pulled at her again. Kate must be seeing this. She must have recognized Tim.

Airlie handed the compact to Tim who took it with his right hand, keeping his left hand in a regular brushing contact with Sooty.

Airlie opened her eyes and closed them again immediately: Tim's view reappeared. She opened them for the count of five, then closed them again: Tim was still managing to maintain the view. And she still had a connection to Kate and Goldie.

Airlie opened her eyes and looked at Sooty on her lap. "Okay, Sooty! This is Tim! He's really very nice and has been giving you a good pat. How about you go and sit on his lap?" She started to stand up and Sooty stood up and looked questioningly up into her face. Tim put the compact in his pocket and shifted closer. He stilled the patting hand as Sooty pushed against it, and brought his right hand close for the cat to sniff, then patted his own lap.

There was another reaction from the link to Kate, and Sooty seemed to feel it too. He seemed to tug on the link to Kate. What could he sense of her? What would he think of Goldie?

Airlie stood up, closed her eyes, tested the links, then moved a couple of steps away from the bed before testing again. Then she moved to her desk. Then she sat down and tested again. She opened her laptop, and tested again. She brought up a map and found the route from Kate's music teacher to her house, and tested again. She searched for a page of Braille combined with Roman characters, and ended up bringing up and capturing the font Braille Neue Standard with black Braille dots over pale blue English characters. Then she tested again.

Tim was actively looking around her room, studying her posters. But most of all studying the back of her head and the glimpse of the laptop screen. She opened her eyes and rolled back her chair, orienting the laptop so they could both see. Except it was too far away.

The right side of the desk was heavy because of the drawers, but the left side was light, and she swung it away from the wall. Sooty opened his eyes to see what was going on, content to stay on Tim's lap. But the screen was still too far away. At least Tim could make out something. She tried to zoom his perspective closer, but he couldn't maintain it while she worked. But at least he could see what she was doing as she edited the font summary to make a six-by-six alphanumeric grid — with the 0 replaced by a space.

But then she pulled up short. The Braille for 1 to 9 was the same as for A to J, and 0 was the same as K not O in Braille. And the dotty backward L thing was a number marker.

"No!" Airlie murmured. "Kate's a smart girl. She'll figure out how to use the standard version."

Then she realized that she hadn't tried talking to Kate. Even though she couldn't answer, she'd get the jerk on the link when she was surprised.

"Kate, can you hear me?" she tried. But she didn't sense any response.

"Tim, maintain your link. I'm going to try to connect my ears to Kate. When I hold up my finger, you try talking to her!"

Airlie connected back to Goldie, careful to avoid disrupting Tim's link to Kate, which she could still sense somehow. Goldie was still blindfolded, and she could somehow hear and feel the emptiness of the room, and maybe a hint of conversation in the background. Or was it a TV? That was worth following up on. There was no sound of music. It could be the news…

She made the connection to Kate and the sense of the room disappeared. There was a sense of discomfort, of wanting to go to the toilet, and Kate was still blindfolded. She tried to reciprocate, to connect her ears to Kate's. It had happened automatically at camp. And had maybe even happened when she'd tried to connect to Inspector Humble and had heard his side of the telephone conversation better than she should have.

She raised her finger and Tim reacted instantly.

"Hello Kate, it's Tim! Can you hear me?"

She felt the tug, opened her eyes and looked at Tim. He didn't seem to have sensed anything, so she stuck up her thumb and nodded enthusiastically. Then she tried.

"Hello Kate, it's Airlie! Can you hear me?

An even bigger tug!

"Can you understand me?"

"Can you see the screen?"

No reaction... No surprise, so no reaction...

"Okay, Tim! I'm going to pick up Sooty now. I want you to keep a hand touching her and me as you transfer to my desk chair, and then I'll put her back on your lap."

That was easier done than said. And now it was time to report. But first...

"Tim, stay here while I leave the room. Try to maintain the connection. Kate, study that six-by-six square and practice spelling out words. The top part is the alphabet, and the bottom part is the numbers — we have different symbols for the numbers unlike Braille. These are a special form of English characters that have Braille dots in them. You'll also be able to see numbers in the clock at the top of the screen, so you can keep track of the time. I want you to practice typing out what you want to say by looking at each letter in turn for about ten seconds. Between words, you'll use the space at the end, two spaces for a comma or colon or whatever, three spaces for end of a sentence or question."

There was a slightly different twinge in the link. Maybe she was a bit confused with all that. *No worries! We'll figure it out!*

Airlie made it down to the lounge without incident, despite closing her eyes every few steps and checking that she and Tim were still connected to Kate visually, although she'd dropped the speech connection. If she were acting as a telephone, it was difficult to play an active role in anything.

"Hi everybody. We've made some progress. Kate and Goldie are now in a house by the feel of it, but are still blindfolded and haven't been given food or a toilet break yet. Goldie can hear some vague conversation, or maybe a TV, in the background. I couldn't make out any words, but I know Goldie's ears aren't tuned well for human speech. Anyway, I'll need to listen a bit more and work on the hearing aspects. That could be important. But for now, I'd like Inspector Humble and Mrs Leskie to go up and talk to her."

Both of them spoke at the same time.

"I'll think about that, but I'll want to ring this info through. That gives us a search radius... I'm not sure what I would say to her." The inspector had already pulled out his phone and started making the call.

"Talk to her... Oh, it will be great to hear her voice... I can't wait!" Kate's mum had already leapt to her feet and was heading for the stairs.

"Wait a minute please Mrs Leskie. You can talk to her through Tim, and she can hear you, but she can't talk back. At the moment, I just want to give her some encouragement, while I'm working on the talking back bit. And Inspector Humble, I want you to encourage her too and talk about the search efforts and ask her to think about things that will help you find her."

"So how is she going to talk back?"

"Two ways. The first way is with keywords or phrases that she can drop naturally when they take her gag off for eating and drinking and toileting. But maybe that's better for questions she should ask them. Anyway, the main way we'll be talking is through typing on the Braille keypad I've made for her. It will take me about half an hour to finish setting that up, so I thought you could talk to her while I'm doing that. But the most important thing is that she doesn't do anything to let them know she's in contact with us."

"There's a lot to think about there," commented Inspector Humble thoughtfully. "I'll give Mrs Leskie a few minutes then I'll talk to her along those lines. But perhaps first up, you should remind her not to give away that we are listening in."

"Yes, I'll do that. It will take a minute to set up the speech link again... I'd like you to wait outside while I go in and establish the link. Then I'd like Mrs Leskie to talk through the doorway to her once I've finished talking, and a minute later walk in so that Tim and Kate can see you. Then after a couple of minutes say goodbye and tell her you'll talk soon. Then the same with Inspector Humble. Controlling it this way helps me track Kate's reactions and know that she can hear you and see you. I'll try to set up the Braille keyboard while you are talking."

It didn't take long to establish the speech connection as she walked up the stairs and she reached across to Tim's vision for a moment too. To her surprise, Tim was carrying Sooty around the room and looking at things and talking about them. Airlie felt Kate's reaction as his voice started to percolate through their connection. She sensed Mrs Leskie and Inspector Humble coming up the stairs behind her as she entered her bedroom.

"Hi Tim! Hi Kate! Kate, it is very important that you don't give away to your captors that you are in any kind of communication with us. They are going to have to give you a food and toilet break soon, and take your gag off. Just don't try talking to us. But do feel free to talk to them and try to get information about them. We'll give you some ideas about that soon. But I'm now going to try to make this Braille Neue keyboard work, and will try to let other people talk to you while I'm doing that."

Airlie moved around Tim to the desk and collected her MacBook and iPad and took them to the bed. She pulled out her expanded BCI kit from the cupboard. Dr Eerdmann had helped her get hold of the extra enhancements they'd used at camp.

She finished setting up the software with the new keypad, so that it would be highlighted with yellow flashes, alternately indicating different rows and columns. She untangled and plugged in the experimental electrodes and got the wireless headset ready.

Not surprisingly, she felt her mind pulled this way and that by Kate and Tim and the people in the room. And the simple tasks she was trying to carry out suddenly became a lot more complex. Surprisingly, she was more distracted by Mrs Leskie's emotional reactions than by the need to hold the speech link open.

She had thought it was going to be difficult keeping a secondary focus on the speech link to Kate. But Tim and Kate's investment in the conversation was doing a brilliant job of keeping it open, and somehow she'd connected in Tim's ears as well as Kate's and could switch her attention between.

The swap over between Mrs Leskie and Inspector Humble didn't exactly go the way she'd tried to orchestrate it though. And she had picked up a lot more emotional reaction from Kate. Maybe letting her mum talk to her hadn't been such a good idea.

Fortunately, Airlie's mum came up to see if she could help and she took Kate's mum downstairs while Inspector Humble came in and introduced himself, and started to give advice. The disruption of the changeover also gave Airlie the chance to give Tim a heads up that she was going to start setting up the EEG gear on his head.

At first, she was concerned that it would distract him, and break the connection, but thankfully he was able to maintain both the audio and video connections without a hitch.

Airlie placed her hand on Sooty's head for a minute, and felt how engaged he was too. She wondered whether he was like that when she was doing her detective investigations. Was she putting too much of a strain on him? Airlie really had no idea just what Sooty's role was in all this, other than being some sort of catalyst.

Finally, everything was set up, the electrodes were calibrated, and the Braille Neue keyboard was flashing on the laptop screen with EEG brainwaves burbling along on the iPad screen.

"Try to type your name, Tim," she told him. "Concentrate on each letter in turn until it comes up, then move to the next one."

He'd got as far as 'T' when they heard a door open — in Kate's room.

Chapter 18

Footsteps approached Kate and then Airlie felt her hood being unstrapped and her gag taken off.

"Who are you? What do you want?" Kate asked.

Airlie opened notepad pages on both screens, and Inspector Humble held up his hand for silence in Airlie's bedroom, then came and crouched down between Airlie and Tim where he could see both screens.

Airlie tried her best to transcribe the kidnapper's words on her pad. "Good to see you're awake. There is no point yelling. Nobody can hear you except for us. And we will treat you well if you behave."

"And I'll treat you much better if I get some explanations, as well as a visit to the toilet and something to eat and drink."

"Ok then! Follow me and we'll arrange all that. Toilet first?"

"Look, you twerp. I'm blind. I'll need the assistance of my dog." Airlie sensed Kate feeling around for Goldie, and then encountering his hood. "You'll need to take his hood off too!"

"I thought that thing on your head was meant to allow you to see."

"Let's just say it's a work in progress. I need my guide dog."

There was a moment of disquiet from Kate, as the kidnapper removed her transceiver headset, but she didn't say anything. There was a slight sound as if he was turning it over in his hands and tapping on it. "There's a magnetic orientation tab on here, but none on your head. This looks like the real deal, but I don't think you've actually got an implant."

Kate said nothing, but Goldie twisted her head from side to side.

"I think the dog's special. What you've been able to do in the last week is well beyond what an occipital implant could allow."

Airlie tried to get down every word of the kidnapper's, but not necessarily all of Kate's. That gave her time to catch up, and the best she could do was jot down some key words or phrases.

"Very well, I will take the dog's hood off. But if he tries to bite anyone, it will go straight back on."

"Guide dogs don't bite. Although normally they don't get put into hoods and muzzles either. Anyway, that's between you and her."

While the kidnapper was taking off Goldie's hood. Airlie tried writing some notes about the guy, kidnapper one as she thought of him. 'K1: Male, sounds like late 30s early 40s. Neutral accent — very precise.'

Tim rattled off something on his keyboard: 'pedantic tone, not from around here'.

Suddenly, she had sight: Goldie's blue and yellow vision. Goldie looked at the kidnapper and then Kate, giving a quiet woof. She held out her hand to her and Goldie obediently walked her hand onto his harness handle, then looked again at the kidnapper who was silhouetted against the doorway.

Airlie wrote 'light off in room, some light coming from blind — sunset — west facing — unfurnished. Light on in living or loungeroom beyond. TV.'

She started a quick sketch of the man's face with her stylus, labelling it 'K1', then tried a quick profile as he turned sideways and stretched out his hand politely to let Kate out.

Kate didn't move till he spoke. "Come on then."

"Ok, Goldie! Forward! Follow! Find the bathroom!"

After minute or two of soft steps through living room with comfy looking lounge chairs and a small dining table with four chairs, but no people, Goldie followed the kidnapper out into a hallway. Kate stayed in her perspective rather than trying to shift it up like Airlie had taught her.

The man stopped at a door, opening it. Goldie stopped for a moment too, poking her head in then guiding Kate into a bathroom. She went in about a meter then stopped, and Goldie looked back at her as she felt around with her left hand.

"Shower and bath on the right. Basin then toilet on the left." The kidnapper was at least trying to be helpful.

"Thank you. I think I can take it from here." Kate made a show of feeling along the basin and then reaching out to find the door, which she then closed. She couldn't find any way to lock it.

Kate had Goldie find the 'seat' then turned her around to face the door. Airlie could sense her annoyance at the absence of a bolt.

After an embarrassing sequence of sounds and smells, Kate got up and headed over to Goldie who looked around as she pulled a bag out of the harness. Then she sidled Goldie up close to the door and opened it.

K1 was waiting outside the door but Kate held the bag out blindly. "Goldie needs to do her business too. And I hope you've got food for her."

"One of my associates is good with dogs, she'll look after her."

"Thank you!"

Once Kate was seated at the table, with Goldie seated obediently beside her, a second kidnapper came to take her out. K2 knew enough to say "Come" and Goldie obediently went, and that made clear that there was a female kidnapper in the team. Accent was again neutral, perhaps foreign though rather than any brand of native English speaker.

The toileting exercise gave Airlie a good opportunity to sketch Kidnapper 2, as she got increasingly frustrated when Goldie just sat next to her or walked obediently next to her, without doing her business, and she got a lot more opportunity to hear her talk, including some likely curse words that Airlie didn't recognize and tried to write down phonetically.

Of course, Airlie knew from Kate that guide dogs were trained not to mess up the place and did their business only on command. At camp, Airlie had gotten to take Goldie on some playtime walks with business opportunities.

138

Airlie could sense Kate struggling to stare straight ahead as she felt her way on with her eating. Airlie and Tim had to keep a straight face too, because if either of them laughed it would set off Kate and give the game away — a very serious game.

It was particularly funny because Goldie was in on the joke too and strangely enough Airlie could actually sense how entertained she was by the proceedings, which was a nice change from the uncertainty and worry she'd been giving off while blindfolded.

Kate had actually used the command word when talking to them, and Goldie had heard it and knew precisely what was going on: the walkers had to learn to use the correct commands, and guide dogs were good at training their walkers!

The other part of the joke was that she wasn't meant to do her business while in harness.

The aim of the exercise was clearly to get Kate and Goldie out together so that Kate could get Goldie to do her 'big business' and 'little business'. Actually 'busy busy' would do just as well for a quick squirt here and there. But as it was, Kate and Airlie and Tim and Goldie got to have a very good look at what seemed to be an ordinary but very quiet suburban neighbourhood.

But there weren't any passers-by, and in Goldie's strange yellow-blue perspective Airlie couldn't make out any street signs. And she didn't hear any dogs barking or traffic noise either. She tried to elevate her perspective, but it got very blurry beyond what she had already seen.

The house was bluey rather than yellowy, which meant it wasn't red, yellow, orange or green, or raw brick for that matter. Although it could perhaps be something like cyan or magenta, but cyan was near enough to blue, and magenta would be just too horrible to imagine. Airlie wrote down that the house seemed to be blue and not brick, and she attempted to sketch the front façade. It seemed to be a bit of an older style, but how old she couldn't guess.

There was a number on the door which she could direct her perspective back to, but it was fuzzy. She could tell it was two digits, with the first one maybe being 1 or 4 or 7 or perhaps a straight 9 — but normally house numbers would use a curly 9. The second digit was probably a 3 or an 8, or maybe a curly 6 or 9. She was sure that neither of them was 0, and pretty sure that the second digit wasn't 2 or 5.

Airlie scanned around in her mind to see if she could spot a house number on the house opposite, but it was too indistinct. But there was a number on the curb that looked like it could be either 50 or 60. She decided it must be 50, which meant that Kate and Goldie were probably in 49, or perhaps 43 — depending how precisely the houses lined up.

She sketched a quick plan of what she'd seen of the street, with a cross street two houses down to the left, and pencilled in her guesses of 49? and 50?

Actually, Airlie thought, *training Kate with the alphabet and digits might also help Goldie distinguish them better.* She hoped that El's alphabet books would have a good range of fonts, and made a note to ask her to see if there were number and digit training readers as well, for learning to count. She'd get Airlie used to the BCI keyboard with the Braille Neue font, and then quickly change that around through a variety of different fonts and styles to help them both build up the appropriate pattern memory.

Maybe Goldie could *learn to read — and count!*

Airlie's thoughts were interrupted by a comment from Kate. "If you're going to wave your hands in front of my face to check that I'm blind, please try not to hit my nose. Also, you should be aware that the breeze is a bit of a giveaway. I don't suppose you've recharged my cortical interface… I hope you haven't broken it. They are very expensive, not to mention rare."

Then she heard K1 again "Leave her alone! She can't see anything at the moment. I checked. Go!"

"Yes, boss!"

Now Airlie could put a voice to K3: sounded youngish — male, early twenties maybe, not particularly confident, and clearly not very well trained. Maybe an amateur team rather than a government team, criminals rather than spies. *That's a lot to read into two words,* Airlie thought. But she noted down her ideas anyway, followed by three question marks! The accent was slightly drawled, but it didn't quite ring true. Maybe he was being funny, sarcastic…

Airlie added a note: 'K3 maybe foreign: accent is not quite right. Or maybe joking around…'

Finally, K2 gave up on Goldie, snapping the plastic bag between her hands. "If you're not going to do your business, we can go back in!"

That triggered an immediate crouch response. K2 jumped back at a sudden sizzle of spray, which Airlie smelt and felt as well as heard. Then Goldie left a couple of solid presents before moving away to the fence, leaving her unwilling servant to do what she liked with it.

Airlie could sense Goldie's air of disdain.

Chapter 19

It wasn't long before K1 took Kate and Goldie back to her room. It was funny how it hung off the side of the dining room but was a bit smaller. It had a heater under a mantelpiece. A gas heater maybe. *I guess Goldie likes heaters when they're on*, Airlie thought.

The kidnappers hadn't put hoods or gags back on either Kate or Goldie.

As soon as the door closed, Airlie spoke aloud to Kate. "Don't say anything, except maybe to talk to Goldie as you normally would. They are probably listening. You can click your teeth to say 'Yes' or 'Okay' or 'I understand', double click for 'No' and triple click for 'I don't know' or 'you've got the wrong idea' or 'that doesn't make sense'... Okay?"

Airlie heard a single click.

"Gotcha! Okay, I'm going to try to withdraw from the audio connection while leaving you linked to Tim so I can concentrate on other things. I'll try to take a look around the house in a moment and then drop the video link too. Then we can see if we can communicate using Tim's BCI. In the meantime, Tim and Inspector Humble will talk to you."

Airlie concentrated on Goldie's vision, letting go of her other senses. The room was dim, although there was a tiny bit of light from a window with the blind down. Focusing Goldie's vision on that it seemed that there was a closed wooden shutter on that. She hadn't noticed it from the outside, but it seems that they were on the right side of the house from the way they'd navigated inside. She pushed her vision through and tried to steer it round to the front. It sharpened up as she did so, but the street was still quiet.

She tried focusing in on house numbers and the side streets, but still couldn't make out any more letters or number clearly. She steered through the front door and then into the dining room. K1 was sitting on a chair right next to the door, his head leaning back and touching the wall. There were three others quietly playing cards and Airlie recognized the K2 woman. There was a twentyish guy who was presumably K3, and another — K4 obviously — who looked to be more like thirty. She couldn't make out the numbers on the cards, but she could distinguish the face cards from the number cards. Odd that she couldn't identify or count the pips.

The house got blurry as she tried to go beyond where Kate and Goldie had been. Strange that she couldn't see places she hadn't been, but could recognize the age of people Goldie hadn't seen — not that she could sketch more than a general sort of face. K1 and K2 both had a proper face, but the other two… When she tried to distinguish eye colour or hair colour, there was none, but the face looked normal even though she couldn't make any judgements other than age.

Maybe they weren't being distinguished by age, but somehow associated. Airlie focused in on Goldie's sense of smell. What could she distinguish about these people by smell. K1 had a musky smell that she recognized, come to think of it. K2 had some sort of flowery perfume that seemed very uninteresting. K3 had some kind of astringent

144

aftershave smell that was absolutely horrid, and didn't really disguise his body odour, which was actually quite interesting to Goldie. K4 had a more mature smell, and a scent that was maybe the residual of some kind of deodorant. Intriguing...

Airlie opened her eyes and made another note. 'Maybe could connect to a police tracker dog and give them the scents. Maybe could connect to Wendy and Cocoa and they could help identify the scents.'

Airlie tuned back to Kate and Goldie and the conversation in the room with Tim and Inspector Humble. There was also a pile of children's alphabet picture books there — she hadn't even noticed El come in.

Tim was saying "Airlie was right. The main kidnapper, the one she calls K1, is sitting right outside your door with his head against the wall. He'll hear anything you say."

"Do you normally say goodnight to Goldie?" Airlie asked. "Does she normally sleep in your bedroom? Can you tell her good night and to go to sleep and then try to focus in on your connection to Tim? Try to connect to him directly rather than through Goldie. Tim will reach out to you from his side."

Goldie obediently lay down and closed her eyes. Airlie felt Kate drop the connection with Goldie and stretch her senses out. Airlie still had her auditory connection but had never managed to connect her sight with her directly. She felt Tim lose the connection to Goldie and seek out another connection. She flicked Kate's connection across to Tim and concentrated on holding it together. It was like directing her attention.

Airlie squeezed her eyes tight. "Tim, close your eyes. Both of you try to steer your attention round this room's soundscape. Can you hear Tim's breathing and heartbeat?"

She focussed her attention on herself.

"What about my breathing, my heart?"

Click!

"Can you sense me on this chair in front of Tim?"

Click!

"Can you steer around to Tim's left and find Inspector Humble?"

Click!

"My bed is behind them! Can you feel the room's ambience, the open door to the inspector's left?"

Click!

As she spoke, as Kate's individual tooth clicks came in, she felt the connections grow stronger. She felt a sense of body heat from the individuals in the room, a sense of draught from the door, and cooking smells, and the inspector's sweaty smells.

"Tim, open your eyes!"

There was a flashing view of herself though from Tim's perspective, but then it was gone. But there was a jolt of surprise from Kate.

"Did you see something Kate?"

Click!

"Did you see me?"

Click!

"Great! As a blind person, your visual-processing real estate tends to be taken over by other senses, and allows for more detailed processing of these other sensory impressions, building the same sort of sense that would normally be driven by vision. I've tried to link those areas between you and Tim. I'm going to take you through that same exercise again, but this time you won't be surprised, and instead you'll try to grasp hold of Tim's vision, and I'll help you."

Click!

"It should be different from Goldie's vision, because dog vision and human vision have different colour systems."

Click!

They tried again, with much the same result. Although maybe Tim's image lasted a second or so.

"Okay, good! We're all getting tired, so I'm going to try something a bit different. This time the idea is to try to recognize Tim's distinctive quantum brain patterns. I want you to be able to connect without me. I'm going to withdraw from you both and I want you to take charge Kate, steer things around the same way you would normally, but using Tim's mind — and click to ask him to open his eyes when you are ready."

Click!

"Withdrawing now. You're on your own."

Click!

Airlie got up and stretched. She maintained just enough sense of Kate and Tim to know they were still connected, picked up her pad and went to the door, catching Inspector Humble's eye and jerking her head towards it. She opened the door and saw that the upstairs corridor was full of people. She put her finger to her lips, but Kate's mum spoke out loudly nonetheless.

"What's happening? When can I talk to her?"

Kate shut the door before saying anything.

"It's not easy, Mrs Leskie. And everyone's getting tired. But Kate is hearing through Tim's ears and is practicing seeing through his eyes. If you go in and sit on my chair opposite Tim she'll see you. But she can't say anything, or she'll alert the kidnappers. Tim can help you ask yes/no questions and relay the answers. I'll let her know you're coming in, as it won't do to surprise her into saying something."

She opened the door and poked her head inside and said quietly. "Tim, Kate! You mum's going to come in and sit where I was. If you find it hard to keep your emotions or reactions under control, or are getting too tired, just click four times and Tim will ask her to leave and we'll start to wrap things up for the night. But the more we practice now, the more your brain can start to rewire overnight. But we'll try to keep a loose connection between you and Tim going. I'm going to get something to eat now, and when I come back Tim can go and have some dinner."

Dinner was very strange! Mum and Dad and Peter were unusually silent, and just listened to the conversation between Airlie, Inspector Humble and Sergeant El Sanford, who had been invited to join them.

"I really don't understand what you're doing," the inspector was saying. "Why is it so important for Tim to be involved? And how can he connect to his sister like that?"

"I think it's just like the quantum physicists and psychologists theorized at camp," Airlie replied. "The collider experiments are creating twinned Calcium atoms and these are in solution in milk, and tend to stay close to each other, because they act the same due to the twinning. But shaking and pouring milk means that in a household they get distributed amongst the younger people who both drink more milk and have more plastic brains. They continue to act similarly and so tend to end up in similar parts of the brain, as well as throughout the body, in the skin and muscle and bone, and in particular throughout the nervous system, in the synapses and the neurons and their myelin sheaths. That creates tuned associations..."

"Yes, I have some vague recollection of all that being discussed. But how does it relate to you and Tim and Kate, and Sooty and Goldie? Why are you so keen to get Tim and Kate connecting? Why can't you just keep on linking to Kate?"

"I was only exposed to the same food as Kate for a few weeks at camp, but Tim has been in the same house with her all his life. There are twinned ions throughout their bodies, and in particular in the visual cortex. Kate's visual cortex is very different from mine, and more tuned now to Goldie's. But there are a huge number of twinned ions in corresponding places in Kate and Tim's brain. But there also ions twinned in other people, or not twinned at all. It's a matter of tuning into those that are in harmony with each other — which is then a two-way street. So Kate needs to develop human vision rather than only understanding the world in a doglike way. At least that's the theory..."

Airlie looked across at the inspector, then across to Sergeant Sanford. The inspector seemed to be nodding rather hesitantly, so Airlie tried to simplify things a bit.

"I'm hoping that by keeping Tim and Kate in tune, she'll develop the ability to see human colours and most importantly, learn to read, and perhaps even learn to communicate telepathically, like we kind of managed at one point on camp."

"How does that work? I thought there was only a mirroring across the sensory, motor and visual parts of the brain?" El interjected.

"Well, one or two times at camp, just before the arrow incident, I managed to unintentionally communicate telepathically with Kate. Her auditory cortex is no doubt very different from mine too. And Professor Eerdmann came up with a theory that mirroring is key here. There are neurons called mirror neurons that react both when you speak and when you hear. They are supposed to be important feedback for language learning. But there are other neurons associated with grammar and meaning and understanding, that mirror unspoken and understood language and actions — allowing the same parts of the brain to be involved for both speaking and understanding language even though they are generally more closely associated with one or the other."

"So how does that help us find Kate?"

"It doesn't directly, but it allows me to get a better look and listen to the kidnappers, to sense them in human terms.

150

It means that Tim can do a lot of the communicating — and he should have much clearer senses with hundreds of times the paired ions. We don't actually get any direct location information. Getting Tim involved frees me up to go searching for clues as to where she is, and if I get into the right neighbourhood, I can then start exploring with my dimensional gift."

"How can you find the right neighbourhood? asked the inspector.

"That's what I hope we can do tomorrow after I've linked up Tim with the EEG. The BCI will provide another way for her to communicate if the telepathy doesn't come good — or perhaps to assist in getting a telepathic link. I'll set up in the morning and show Peter and Tim what to do. Also the BCI might be useful for tracking her movements on a map. But they seem to be lying low for the moment, so tomorrow I want to track her movements in a convoy with the same kinds of vehicle as the kidnappers, starting from the time of her kidnap."

Dad had a question at this point. "What happened to the satellite tracking, Inspector? Haven't they been able to track them at all?"

"Ahh! It's a misconception that there are satellites watching everywhere all the time. We haven't managed to track down any satellites that were tasked to the neighbourhood at the time of the kidnap. Drones and helicopters also didn't manage to spot any suspicious black vehicles, let alone convoys. Nor did our patrol cars."

Chapter 20

Airlie had a restless night, running Goldie's memory of the kidnapping through in her mind over and over again until she got up in despair of getting to sleep and tried to track the route on a map. But it was too complicated: there were too many nearby streets that went in different ways.

Eventually she gave up and went to bed, then slept in till after eight, and raced down to breakfast to find additional guests. Peter and Tim had already finished, and Tim was excited that he'd managed his connection to Kate and Goldie without Airlie's help.

Kate was finishing up breakfast by herself apart from the close scrutiny of K1, which she was doing her best to ignore. Goldie, however, was acting quite suspicious towards him, and she ignored K2 when she came in and placed bowls of food and water near the door, sniffing disdainfully.

"You must have chosen one of the cheaper brands," Kate commented. "Goldie can be quite fussy. But she'll probably have some after she's had her toilet break and I've had mine. Also, it would be nice to have a shower and a change of clothes. This kidnapping business is not as exciting as I'd have expected. Are you going to keep me locked up till I die of boredom?"

"My colleague has put a change of clothes in the bathroom for you. She thinks she has got the right sizes. You are welcome to use the facilities now. And you can expect to have some visitors in about an hour. That should relieve the boredom for a while."

"Thank you. I can manage on my own now I know my way around, so it would be good if Goldie can have her toilet break now."

Airlie and Tim dropped their connection to Kate while she completed her toiletries and Kid2 took Goldie out. That gave her opportunity to welcome her visitors.

"Hi, Dr Eerdmann! I didn't know you'd be coming."

"Hello Airlie! I was so sorry to hear about Kate and Goldie, and Inspector Humble thought you and Tim could do with some help with the BCI. It sounds like you've got a few ideas, and have already made some progress."

Airlie and Tim reported on the conversation with K1, and Inspector Humble was keen to strategize. He wanted Kate to be reasonably cooperative with them, but to ask questions and play ignorant, delaying things, avoiding giving anything away about the quantum talents. What did they know? How did they know?

"She'll have to be careful. It will be a dance, with everyone trying to trick Kate into giving away something, even making believe they know things they don't. Conversely Kate will be trying to get information out of them, but it will be many against one — as far as they know. Hopefully, we can balance up those odds."

"Yes, and she shouldn't connect to Goldie. She should be the blind girl. Tim can now connect to Kate directly, and I'll want to have access to Goldie."

"Do you have access to a quiet drone?" Airlie asked the inspector as they drove to Kate's music teacher's place.

"What do you mean?"

"I mean, do you have a drone that can follow a vehicle without being heard."

"Of course! Some of them can track from a distance and would be impossible to see or hear from inside a car."

"Will I be able to see its video live from inside the truck?"

"No problem! The truck I've got for us is a surveillance van. We'll have Minor Affairs people driving the van and operating the drones — two drones at a time."

They arrived at the kidnap point amid a cluster of police vehicles, but there was no truck.

"It will join us and pick us up the same way Kate was kidnapped. But don't let your expectations get too high. Traffic noise won't be the same, so it will be hard to know when you're tracking properly."

"Right. Let's think of this as a dress rehearsal," Airlie suggested, as they started walking Kate's route. "We'll probably want to do a second run later, at the same time Kate and Goldie were taken. The traffic will be more similar then."

Two police cars and a van screeched around the corner and pulled up beside them. People emerged from all three vehicles, some uniformed some not, and bundled Airlie and the inspector into the van.

There were two people inside with screens, but they didn't say anything, just exchanged quick nods with the inspector and Airlie before returning their attention to the drones they were controlling. There wasn't much space and they'd just strapped in on the sideways benches, when El's voice came from the front via an intercom: "Say when!"

Airlie closed her eyes and connected with Goldie and tracked her back to the point when the vans arrived. "They didn't arrive with a screech of brakes. We need to proceed more sedately. Goldie was facing forward and Kate was facing her… She's put her arm around me, like cuddling me… umm, her! Ok, go!"

Airlie heard the car in front start off. She wasn't sure how orders were relayed to the other cars.

Goldie felt the vehicle slow, and then pick up speed again, subtly adjusting her balance. "Go through this intersection," Airlie instructed. They heard the front car drive off again, but even Goldie's ears weren't good enough to hear the one behind.

The van slowed again, and this time she felt herself pulled to the right. "Turn left."

Following the turns was surprisingly easy, although one or other van had to slow at various times, and lane changes were tricky to pick up and quick manoeuvres were needed for Humble's van to make the turns. Although at least Goldie's sensitive ears could hear the blinker. *Interesting, because I can't in this van.*

"Okay, slowing again… another intersection I guess… stopping."

"No, no intersection," El responded. "We're in a tunnel."

Airlie listened carefully. "There are people getting out. Something is being dragged past me, past Goldie. But Goldie can still sense Kate... There's the sound of slapping and scraping against the side panels, and the roof. They're getting back in... Moving off... Wait..."

There was something different now. But Kate couldn't put her finger on it. The tone of the driving sounds had changed. *Was it the tunnel?*

Airlie rewound and paid attention to the sound. There was a different, louder, harsher sound from the outside. "Something's different. There's a shushing type of sound because of the tunnel I think. But there's something else."

Inspector Humble replied. "That would be increased echo of the tyre noise. That will sound like white noise."

"I suppose. No, there's something else. Even that is different now they're moving again: more muffled."

"I suspect they've put on some magnetic advertising panels or logos," suggested the inspector. "Maybe changed the colour of the roof."

Airlie replayed the tunnel entry, stop, restart and exit again. "I think you're right. But there's something else different. Goldie can hear all the expected vehicle sounds just as loudly, but somehow a bit deader."

"Losing the high frequency," the senior drone operator said — Mick, Airlie recalled. "Like you said, muffled by the panels."

"No that's still not everything. There's something missing... I know! There's no sound of the car in front moving off." Airlie went over it again, listening carefully.

"Sounds like they were ready for the drone surveillance," Mick concluded. "The search for three black vehicles is just too easy — that's no doubt why we didn't pick them up while they were *en route* to their safe house."

After that, speeds picked up as they entered the outer reaches of the city. But eventually they needed to turn right and there was no road or property to turn into.

It turned out there were roads around half a kilometre ahead and behind them. Their driver had been doing the speed limit which was 80 km/h along there, and everyone seemed to have different views about whether it was more likely the kidnappers would have driven above or below the speed limit.

"They would have kept below the speed limit," proposed Humble. "They'd stand out less and wouldn't get stopped for speeding."

"Actually," said Mike, "they'd stand out more, because the traffic along here regularly does a bit more than the limit, and there are rarely any speed traps on this stretch."

Their driver, Phil, thought both were wrong. "The correct thing to do is drive at the speed limit, which is what I did. So it's more likely we went wrong earlier — somewhere between the tunnel and here. I think we can all agree that that fits too perfectly for us to have gone off track earlier."

In the end the drone operators explored both the side roads in parallel at 80 km/h, which was both the drones' maximum speed and the speed limit on those roads. But neither avenue fitted at all with Goldie's memories.

It was all very disappointing, but Airlie hadn't really expected it to work out first time. With the tunnel discoveries, they'd really done very well, and the inspector was very upbeat about progress and was initiating on-the-ground enquiries to see if anyone had seen the van in its new guise — a very vague idea of a van with a logo on the side.

They decided to return to the tunnel, calculating that the van had reached there about 25 minutes after the kidnapping, plus or minus a couple of minutes. Inspector Humble was confident that the kidnappers had been there, and had a forensics team out looking for any evidence of the stop or the other vehicles in the convoy.

Even though it was a bit out of the way, there could have been hundreds, even thousands, of vehicles through there in the last 24 hours, so Airlie didn't expect them to find anything and didn't pay much attention to the team of people in their orange suits. Rather she wandered around the tunnel and up the steps to the railway line overhead.

There weren't any trains in sight, but there was a footpath along one side of the track and she took in as much of the landscape as possible, trying to attend to every little detail of her 360° panorama. As she'd done with the Luna case, she tried to cast her memory and imagination back to the time of the incident and visualize the truck. But it wasn't working.

But last time, she'd had Sooty on her lap, patting her as she thought over the day, and holding her quite tightly as she envisaged the dognapper's van.

They were 20-25km away from Sooty at the moment: more than 25 by road, but quite a bit less as the crow flies. But distance didn't seem to make a lot of difference with Airlie's telepathic gifts, so she tried to connect to Sooty.

Airlie never actually felt she was Sooty, like she shared Goldie's sensorimotor experiences. But there was that click of connection. She suddenly found herself in her bedroom, looking at Sooty on the bed.

Sooty opened her eyes and stared straight into her virtual eyes, and the connection seemed to deepen.

Airlie started out for Kate's place and the crime scene, then sent her imagination back to see the vehicles. She followed them out along the route they'd taken, but it was still blurry.

Of course, she'd been in the back of the van and couldn't see anything. She'd planned to ride back in the front and take note of the route they were passing through. They'd need to leave pretty soon to get back in time to start the route exactly 24 hours after the kidnapping.

But she pushed on anyway.

Airlie connected back into Goldie's route memory and pulled herself along it to her location at the railway overpass. Suddenly things began to unblur and she saw the three vehicles approaching in the distance. They kept coming, two black sedans, and passed underneath her.

She turned around, physically as well as mentally, seeing one black car come out.

Airlie waited and waited. *Was that it?*

She pushed forward and envisaged the altered van coming out. A white bonnet emerged, followed by a white roof. She backed away in her mind to see the sides. The logo wasn't clear but she had the impression of blue and orange writing which she tried to decipher letter by letter. No, it was blue writing, and some sort of cartoon image in orange — sort of like someone vacuuming between the words, the words that she couldn't make out.

But maybe it was 'Carpet Cleaning'? *Somebody or other carpet cleaning.* The words 'Carpet Cleaning' seemed to fit, seemed to take shape, but there were other words, a stylized logo in orange above it. *One word,* she thought.

Airlie started down to let Inspector Humble know, but then remembered the trailing vehicle. She watched the carpet van move out of sight, noting how that same orange logo seemed to be split across the van's rear doors. Only once it was out of sight did the trailing black car emerge. She watched it slow at the first crossroad and turn right.

Airlie opened her eyes and pulled herself back to the present, to find Inspector Humble standing near the top of the steps, watching her.

"What have you seen?" he asked.

"The fake panels are white with blue text and an orange logo and cartoon. I think the blue text says 'Carpet Cleaning' and the cartoon is someone vacuuming, but I can't get the logo. I think I might get more if I watched them put the panels on from in the tunnel."

They went down the steps together, and Airlie saw that the forensics unit had gone. "I don't suppose they found anything?" she offered.

"Actually, they didn't do too badly. Of course, with a couple of hundred cars a day going through, they didn't find anything on the road. But it seems the kidnappers did pull to the side a little and there's a track and some footsteps apparent around the edge of the road seal. The bitumen doesn't go right to the edge."

"Ok, well let's have a peek."

Airlie walked into the tunnel a short way. It was just long enough to fit the van and the car, with not enough room for the front car. So, the van would have been at the front.

She wound her mind back and watched it come in and stop, the rear vehicle pulling up a metre or so behind and actually sticking out of the tunnel a bit.

The passenger and driver's doors opened. She recognized the passenger as K1 and the driver was probably K3. The back of the van was flung opened, and she saw K1 give K2 an annoyed look as she appeared around the side of a spreadeagled door. The three of them manhandled out a big white cut out in the shape of the side of the van, and stuck it on to the van like a fridge magnet. They did the same on the other side.

Airlie commentated to the inspector as she watched.

They finished off with smaller panels for the hood and the roof, and then K2 got back into the van and gently shut the rear doors. K1 applied the rear panels and quietly got back into the van. It drove off.

"Four minutes and thirty-seven seconds: that's efficient, and well-practised," Humble commented.

But Airlie still couldn't make out the name of the company, apart from the 'Carpet Cleaning' part that seemed completely clear now.

"Maybe if I did some research on the web, I could pick up the name." Airlie suggested.

162

"Maybe later," Humble answered. "I think this is plenty to get sensible information from people in the area. It could well be a fake company. Certainly, it won't be anything to do with them. But let's have something to eat before continuing on from here."

This time Airlie sat in the front of the van, squeezed between Inspector Humble and Sergeant Sanford. El was driving and the inspector had recorded the timings from the last run through, and set a timer countdown on his phone that they could all see.

So Airlie was free to look around and get a feel for the outer suburbs they were driving through, some of them clearly country towns that had been absorbed into the metropolis. For her to change her perspective viewpoint, it seemed she needed a solid starting point. But she didn't have a good explanation of why that might be: it was more than just changing a visual perspective because there was the time aspect, but maybe there was some sort of quantum twinning going on, though she had no idea how that could be.

Something to talk about to the quantum physicists... But for now, she practiced moving the time forward and confirmed that the van had come this way. But she still couldn't make out the name of the company. It just looked like a zigzag with parallel lines at the end. Maybe the zigzag was an M or a W, maybe with an A in there somewhere?

El interrupted her thoughts. "The traffic is a bit heavier now, so we're moving a bit more slowly. We're coming up to the turn before the one we got to last time, but still have over a minute on the clock. Should I take it?"

Airlie tried to do her time warping exploration around the intersection, as El slowed.

"Sounds like a reasonable idea," answered the inspector thoughtfully.

"Actually, can we just stop there for a while without making the turn? I'm trying to get back to when the kidnappers were here."

The inspector agreed and radioed the lead car to stop and pull over. They were continuing in convoy even though the kidnappers had split up, and they were used to the rear car taking point and the front car pulling in behind whenever it got ahead of an unexpected turn.

"Ok, I've got them, and they seem to be turning here. I hope it's not just my imagination. How about we set the next time just in case, but I'll try to track them."

But once again, she somehow lost it. It was as if her attention was jolted when they got beyond the horizon, when she saw the new scene ahead, and then the carpet cleaning van just wasn't there. It was strange too how the carpet cleaning words, and the cartoon cleaner, were so clear now, but the rest of it just wouldn't focus. And the number plate was a complete blur too: there was a hint of characters, but she couldn't even say which were letters and which were numbers. Even the colours were indistinct, bluey and yellowy.

"I'm sure Goldie got a glimpse of the number plate, but it's still not resolving into anything useful. Hopefully Tim is getting the opportunity to teach Kate and Goldie their letters and numbers. That might help, but it's a long shot even before considering whether it could work retrospectively."

As the time announcing the next left turn was approaching, a street came up, and they repeated the process. The lead car went around, and Airlie had a good look around before closing her eyes and trying to bring the image of the cleaner van back again. It took only a few seconds for it to move into view.

Airlie tried opening and closing her eyes every few seconds to update her surrounds and keep track of the pseudomemory trace. But again she lost it.

"Garghh!" she muttered in exasperation.

"What do you mean, 'Garghh'?" El asked, "You're doing fantastic. We're tracking an invisible van as far as I'm concerned."

They were almost out in the country now, and passing through a bushy cross between a suburb and a town, complete with petrol pump and general store.

The inspector ordered the trailing car to pull in and interview the people there. "It's a long shot," he commented "but if we can just get a witness to confirm seeing a carpet cleaning van, I'd be so much more confident we are on the right track."

"Not to mention having some real evidence and witnesses that could actually be brought into court," added El sardonically.

It didn't pan out. But every new town they passed, they repeated the process and eventually they hit paydirt.

The cop radioed the news through. "The owner and a customer at the pump actually had a conversation about it. They thought it odd to see a strange carpet cleaner in the area when all the locals used Menno's, who are just round the corner off the main road."

"Excellent," responded the inspector. "Get as good a description of the van as you can. In fact, get the witnesses to go round to this Menno's and discuss it with them and see if it rings any bells. Someone in the business should know their competition. If there are other people who might have seen it, try to find out. I don't know that door-to-door canvassing really makes much sense in this area, so be guided by the locals."

Chapter 21

Airlie! Airlie, I need you!

I'm here Kate! Can you hear me?

Airlie snapped into Goldie's present and Kate's senses came alive too, and Tim was there somewhere in the background. Kate and Goldie were just being ushered back to their room, but she could hear vehicles drawing up, doors slamming outside, and a peremptory voice giving orders.

Airlie, thank God! There are more people arriving. Lots of people, lots of vehicles.

"Inspector," Airlie said out loud. "Kate's…"

The inspector held up his hand as a call came in, listening and making grunting noises before starting to give orders. But Airlie was too focused on Kate to pay attention, and at that moment Kate's door opened and a crying girl and a bewildered dog were ushered in by K1: a girl and a dog she hadn't seen before.

"I'll leave you two to get acquainted," the kidnapper said before leaving and slamming the door behind him.

The strange girl jumped, but the two dogs were more focused on each other. They were both service dogs. It almost seemed like they recognized each other professionally. They were both in working mode of course.

"Urgh… Hi! I'm Kate…"

Give both names, Airlie thought at her.

"Kate Leskie," Kate continued, moving closer, putting an arm around her and sitting down with her on the couch she'd been using as a bed.

The girl looked closely at her, wiping tears from her eyes, and Kate tried again.

"Hi! What's your name? I'm Kate, Kate Leskie and this is Goldie!"

"Libby and Fringe," the girl sobbed back in a strange accent. "Elizabeth Fenton... I'm deaf and can only lipread you when I look at you, or ... What's going on here? Where are we? You're not one of them, are you?"

"No, Goldie and I were kidnapped too... at least I'm assuming you were."

Libby nodded, but Kate continued on as if she hadn't noticed. "I'm blind, so I can't lipread at all, and I can't see any gestures you make, so you have to talk in words: spell things out."

"Oh, right! I didn't put it together. So your dog is a guide dog, while mine is a hearing dog."

"As to where we are, I don't really know. We drove for well over an hour so are probably on the other side of the city, or even in the country."

"Oh! I'm from Bordertown, and from the traffic... from the way Fringe reacted... and since it's been hours, and I'm getting quite hungry, I'd say we're close to the city, in the hills somewhere."

"Right. Do you know why you've been taken? Are you rich or something?"

168

"Far from rich. No idea really, except... I think it may really be Fringe they want..."

"They're probably listening. And they do feed us... So they'll hopefully come any second to get us for dinner and a toilet break. Although they did have a bit of trouble with Goldie and her toileting. They also have some idea that Goldie is special and that he and I have a special relationship. And they don't believe my cortical implant works... It isn't charged at the moment of course."

Kate and Libby looked at each other, reading the hidden subtexts of their conversation no doubt, then Kate pulled out her cortical interface from her waist pouch and put it on to show her. It was like a pair of heavy-framed glasses with a band that went around the back of her head. As K1 had noticed, there were electrodes in the band as well as magnets in the frame that were meant to help align it with the internal implant.

But then a thought occurred to Kate. "From your accent, I'd guess you were deaf from birth. I thought they implanted children with cochlear implants as babies these days."

"Yes and no," responded Libby. "In my case, the auditory nerves didn't develop fully so the cochlear implant wouldn't work. But there are now auditory brain stem interfaces. Of course, I was too young, and not in an eligible group for the approved prosthetic, and then too old for the clinical trial on children."

"Oh wow," exclaimed Kate. "That's just like with me. A retinal interface was 'contraindicated', and I needed special approval to 'trial' the cortical prosthetic."

Suddenly Airlie was aware that Inspector Humble was waving at her, trying to attract her attention. When she met his eyes, he touched his ear and pointed forward, raising an eyebrow.

Airlie severed the link to Goldie but maintained the telepathic link with Kate.

Hang in there! She relayed. We're making *progress! We're getting close! I'm in a van with the inspector looking for you. We've just come into a significant township and are passing a school.*

OK, Thanks. I'm getting worried. Sounds like they are bringing in lots of equipment.

Airlie felt strangely affected by Kate's rising fear in the face of Libby's ongoing terror, and hadn't really registered the background sounds. She calmed herself deliberately as she turned her attention to the inspector, trying to get her head around everything before she spoke.

"Kate managed to contact me telepathically and Tim has still got a sensory connection with Goldie. They've kidnapped another girl and her hearing dog from Bordertown: an Elizabeth Fenton — goes by Libby. The girl isn't in a good state, and Kate is getting emotional now too. They've been bringing in equipment. I've told her we're in the van looking for her and getting close."

"That explains a few things."

The inspector consulted his Android pad as he continued: "A drone spotted a group of vehicles coming off the expressway, and the middle one was a carpet cleaning van like you described. The clichéd Acme Carpet Cleaning, to be precise. There were two black SUVs that swapped places on the freeway, and then followed parallel routes to a house where they joined a maroon Camry and a white single-cab HiLux that was being unloaded. We got all their number plates, before all but the Camry disappeared. Plus, we have a drone tracking the HiLux and have patrol cars on the lookout for the others. Our other drone has been deployed to watch the house, where two subjects in dark clothes brought a girl and a dog out of the Acme van, and took them to the door of a house, where they were met by a man in a grey business suit."

"Wow!" was all Airlie could manage.

"We're only ten minutes away, less now we're flashing our lights, and we've already got local police from several stations cordoning off the area, and *en route* we have further units from Minor Affairs as well as tactical and negotiation teams from the Kidnapping and Extortion Unit. We'll be coming in without sirens and will rendezvous a couple of blocks away."

The inspector tapped on his tablet and started a video going.

"Here's the drone footage. Look familiar?"

Indeed it did! It fitted exactly with what she'd seen through Goldie's eyes.

Airlie suddenly felt a stab of shock from Kate.

She flashed into Goldie's viewpoint and didn't see why at first. Goldie and Kate were looking at a whole set of EEG gear being set up on the table. It was medical grade stuff, with a skull-style setup that looked to have about 100 electrodes.

They were plugged into three portable amplifiers: each looked like it was 32 electrodes.

Calm down! You're not supposed to be seeing this. It's only EEG equipment, she flashed to Kate.

Then Kate flicked her attention to a sideboard Airlie hadn't noticed before. Another kidnapper was laying out all sorts of medical gear including scalpels and scissors, a drill, and something that looked like some kind of saw.

Oh! Airlie sent. *That doesn't look good. But Libby can see it. Goldie can sense that she's getting agitated. Ask her what's wrong, what they are doing.*

Goldie gave a whimper of agreement, and Kate put her hand down and patted her head for some mutual comfort.

"Libby," Kate called out in a stage whisper. "What are they doing? What's upsetting you? What are they bringing in?" Airlie hoped that Libby was looking at Kate and didn't give away her hearing dog connection.

"They've got all sorts of electrical stuff that they are going to put in our heads. They've got drills and shavers and saws and knives and stuff." Libby responded promptly.

"There is nothing for you to worry about if you are cooperative." Airlie recognized K1's voice, his accent sounding slightly stronger than usual. "The EEG equipment is non-invasive. It just sits on your scalp. Of course, if either of you really have implants, we'll want to have a look at that. And if the EEG doesn't work, we've got ECoG electrodes that actually sit inside your skull on the surface of your brain. But still we've got an experienced medtech. He has been practicing on cadavers... and he has *not* killed any yet."

"I told you I don't have any implants." Libby responded.

"So you say. But your friend is supposed to have an implant. We might just need to check that."

Airlie glanced out the window to see a pub that was evidently the rendezvous point, given the number of police cars in the car park and the big van that was pulled onto the verge ahead of them.

But El turned onto the side street and kept on driving.

Hang in there Kate! Airlie sent. *We're only a couple of minutes out. We're just turning off the main road. Don't say anything. We'll be there before they've even got the EEG wired up. There's no way that can try any brain surgery before we get there.*

Chapter 22

With the distraction, Airlie had to rewind and retry the final bit of Goldie's kidnap memory, but they seemed to be driving exactly the route they took to their safehouse. It gelled perfectly with the inspector's directions on his phone. Glancing at it, the map seemed to resonate with her. They really should be there now.

Airlie looked out the window just as they passed by the house, and everything snapped into place for her. She recognized the house and yard, and was now able to shift her view around the neighbourhood.

"Keep your contact with Kate," the inspector ordered. "Just let her know we know where she is and are close."

They pulled up next to a fleet of other police cars, and the inspector got out, removed his jacket and put on a bulletproof vest, before putting the jacket back on and putting some sort of plug thing into his ear.

Now Airlie was worried! And she was feeling increasing levels of worry filtering through from Kate.

We just passed the house, Airlie told her.

"Can you track me back to the house while still keeping your telepathic link and Kate ears open?" the inspector asked.

"Yes, I'm sure I can. The links stay there pretty automatically once they're open, as long as I look in on them periodically and don't get too distracted."

"OK! I'm going to knock on the front door, and I have a tactical squad surrounding the house ready to move in. They have your sketched plan of the house. Sergeant Sanford will wait here with you and help coordinate things from the van, and we'll keep the drones up monitoring the situation as well. You can keep tabs on the girls, and work with El to keep them safe during ingress. I know you haven't seen any firearms, but I'd be surprised if they weren't armed."

El looked a bit put out at first, but then seemed to relish the coordination role as they moved into the back of the van with the drone operators.

The inspector's heading for the front door, and an attack team is getting in place all round the house, Airlie telemitted.

Airlie slipped back into Goldie's head to find she was being wired up for EEG, and was not liking it one bit, growling and snapping at the operator working on her. She saw someone reach for a syringe, and squirt out a little. As the acrid smell reached Goldie's nose, she reacted instinctively. "Quiet Goldie! Working! Watch out for Kate!"

She must have transmitted that to Kate too, who put her hand on Goldie's head and repeated "Quiet Goldie! Working!"

K5 completed the setup without further trouble, explaining again that it was 'totally non-invasive' and was 'just to see what kind of connection she had with the dog', while K6 continued to hold the syringe in readiness.

When K5 released her head, Goldie pulled back a step and continued to keep a close eye on K6 and that syringe, growling deep in her throat. Airlie could feel the tight EEG cap on Goldie's head. They must have got a special dog one. She pulled back her view to have a look at it.

Suddenly she sensed Goldie starting to raise a paw to pull off the cap. "Stay still Goldie," she said, deliberately telemitting to Kate as well. "Working!"

Again Kate echoed Airlie's commands to Goldie, hugging him close while avoiding the cap and the dozens of leads. Airlie noted that they only had two amplifiers for Goldie: 64 electrodes instead of the 96 they had on Kate.

Kate's breathing was rough, and her anxiety levels were through the roof. But she'd had the presence of mind to disconnect from Goldie, although Goldie was still hypersensitive to Kate's breathing, sweat, heartrate and other vibes that told of how distressed she was.

K5 was now monitoring Kate and Goldie on a pair of laptops connect to the two amplifier rigs. There were extra wires between them that Airlie thought must have been to make sure they were in sync.

"Calm down," ordered K5. "Close your eyes, and breathe deeply and slowly."

Kate shut her eyes and took the required breaths. "Match your breaths to the dog's, and then try to slow both your breath and hers down together.

With Kate and Goldie calming down, Airlie took the opportunity to pull back her view and look around.

Libby and her hearing ear dog were in the room too, sitting up the other end of the table watching, and a lot calmer than they'd been earlier. Airlie guessed the idea was for Libby to know what to expect, since Kate had been there longer and had originally been the calmer of the two.

Airlie circled around the room to take a look at the laptops. She could see the typical artefacts due to heartbeat and breathing, and just disappearing off screen were the tell tales of the closing and opening eyes test, in terms of the EOG, but without the typical eyes-closed alpha rhythm. Although there was a fair bit of activity even in the visual parts of the brain at the back of the head.

"It doesn't seem like she can see at all." K5 explained to the room. "These are typical readings for a blind person and there's no evidence of any injected signals."

Airlie explained the situation to El, and they came up with a plan.

Kate, she relayed. *Inspector Humble will knock on the front door in two minutes and ask about you. Look at Libby and just mouth the words that she should link with her dog, and you can link with Goldie too. That should distract them with a bit of excitement. The inspector will tell them the house is surrounded and they are under arrest. The word 'arrest' is your signal. If they try to gag you or restrain you before that, struggle and yell — and that's our signal. Either way, that's the time for all of you to yell and yell and bark and bark and get under the table. It's a signal for the armed team as well, so there will soon be other distractions for your kidnappers. Main thing is get down and stay down.*

'Link with your dog' Kate mouthed as she linked in with Goldie, Airlie and Tim. She shifted Goldie's perspective to her own and caught Libby's surprised eyes staring at her. She nodded, and at the same time there were excited yells from the technicians at the table. "Their occipital lobes are in sync. The girl and the dog, their V1s suddenly jumped to over 60% correlation."

The kidnappers looked up from their phones and their fingernail cleaning. "That's the primary visual cortex," K5 was explaining to the others when the doorbell went.

K1 jumped to his feet, looking frazzled for the first time, dithering around as if he didn't know whether to come or go.

"Probably a salesman," opined K2. "There is a car outside, so they'll assume somebody is home."

"Keep the kids and the dogs quiet," ordered K1. "You can gag them or sedate them if they're unruly, although there are several walls and a solid door between here and the front of the house".

Airlie followed K1 with her virtual eyes, as he went to the door, keeping her ears focussed on Goldie back in the dining room.

The door opened and she saw the inspector confronting K1, and glimpsed someone else in a smart suit standing to one side on the step below him. As she recognized the street outside, her vision snapped out of doggy mode into glorious technicolour. She zoomed around the house and looked in all the windows, even those with curtains, and she spotted the snipers with the green glow of their infra-red scopes reflecting off them.

"I've managed to scry round the house but can't spot anyone outside of the dining room," Airlie reported over the comms. "Wait, there are some people in the room next to it, just to the front of it."

"Good evening! My name is Inspector Humble, Minor Affairs..." K1 seemed to freeze for a moment while the inspector calmly showed his badge, and some photos. "And this is Agent Kim from the Kidnapping and Extortion Unit. We're looking for two kidnapped children and their service dogs. May we come in?"

"I do not see why that is necessary," responded K1 in a matching tone of overpoliteness. "I have not seen any missing children or dogs."

"The girls and the dogs are both in the dining room, but are being threatened with syringes," interspersed Airlie through the comms.

"I have good information that they are in this house, including drone footage. I should also mention we have snipers in place, and that despite the curtains, we can tell you have the children in the dining room. And it seems some of your people are currently threatening them with syringes. Threatening of minors warrants a charge of serious aggravated kidnapping."

K1 took a step back, and Agent Kim moved up beside the inspector and took over seamlessly at that point. "What we don't know is what you want with them. At this stage we would just like to verify their safety and talk. Please, after you!" Agent Kim gestured open handed down the hallway as if she were the host and K1 the guest.

Right then, El got a message on her screen, and relayed it through to the Minor Affairs personnel. "We've just heard back that this house, and all of those around it, are owned by a complicated series of offshore shell companies. So it does look like there are foreign agents involved, although whether government or corporate is unclear at this stage."

K1 seemed to recognize the negotiator's tactics and fell into a suave diplomatic persona, maybe sounding just a bit more foreign too. "Of course, do come this way."

He stepped to the front and halfway down the hall, stopping at a door on their right, and mirrored Agent Kim's earlier gesture to invite them to enter as he reached to open it.

"No!" yelled Airlie into the comms. "That's the wrong room — and the goons in there are getting up... going for guns."

As K1 opened the door at full stretch and politely stayed out of their way, Humble and Kim pulled back from the doorway — just in time to avoid a hail of bullets accompanied by two sharp cracks and a tinkle of glass... then a sudden overwhelming silence. They both drew their own guns and aimed them at K1.

"Thank you," said the inspector, "but we'll try the next one." He walked past the open doorway to the closed door at the end of the hall, waiting back against the wall, until Airlie confirmed that was the one. He shifted the gun to his left hand, then with his right hand reached to the doorknob, turned it and pushed it open, raising his voice and addressing the room from the hallway.

But Airlie was distracted from following the inspector as K1 called out plaintively, "You can't arrest me: I have diplomatic immunity."

She pulled back so she could see K1 and Agent Kim, who responded in polite but firm tones as she pulled out a pair of handcuffs. "I'd be more worried about the snipers outside. It's leave in cuffs or leave in a body bag, I suspect." She pushed K1 against the wall with her gun hand, and somehow managed to cuff him with the other.

Then Airlie's attention shifted back to what the inspector was saying. "The house is surrounded by our tactical unit, with snipers targeting you through the windows. As you might have heard, anyone drawing a weapon will be shot, and that includes anyone still wielding a syringe in three seconds time. You are all under arrest for kidnapping."

There was a clatter of syringes hitting the floor, and a swarm of armed tactical officers slipped in from the hallway behind them, taking positions around the room and covering the kidnappers and technicians from every angle. As others crashed in through the back door and spread out throughout the house, Airlie instinctively pulled up into a bird's eye view that somehow managed to track everyone despite roof, ceilings, and walls.

In no time at all the operation was complete and the kidnappers were being led out in handcuffs, leaving KEU to bag a variety of weapons and Minor Affairs to deal with the EEG and medical equipment.

Chapter 23

Airlie and Kate now had a police car stationed permanently outside of their homes, sometimes two, and one would follow them to their various activities. Most of the officers were familiar to Airlie from the raid, partnering tactically trained specialists from KEU and Minor Affairs personnel — with whatever special training they got. Apparently, Libby's parents were only just starting to worry about her when the police rang, but she was getting the same protection now too.

Airlie's parents invited Inspector Humble and Sergeant Sanford to dinner along with Kate and Tim and their parents, insisting that they were part of the same family now, after all that had happened. So three days after the rescue, they grilled the inspector about the latest developments. He told them what he could.

Tim was very disappointed that he hadn't got to witness firsthand, through Goldie's eyes, a real live-fire SWAT action — complaining that it wasn't at all like on TV.

"Reality is somewhat different," explained the inspector. "In real life, a successful operation is one in which the perpetrators are captured, the hostages are released safely, and nobody is injured. Ideally, not a shot is fired... And that is what 98% of our tactical operations are like."

"Yeah, the paperwork is really something if you fire your weapon," complained El sourly. "Not to mention the after-action reports, the interviews and the counselling if someone actually gets hurt."

But eventually, they got back on topic. "Who were the kidnappers? What did they want? How did they find out about us? What were they going to do with us?" Kate pressed.

Airlie and Tim had been right, the kidnappers were foreign, but the inspector wouldn't be drawn about which country was involved. Airlie's K1 and K2 were indeed consular officials, and the rest of Kate and Libby's abductors (including some identified only from drone footage) also had diplomatic immunity — except for the scientists, who had been brought into the country specially. This had severely limited the investigation as the embassy had declined to waive immunity for their personnel. This was taken by Foreign Affairs to imply that the operation had been sanctioned by their government, if not actually run by one of their agencies.

Still the so-called diplomats were being expelled — and the two scientists were facing multiple charges but were being quite cooperative in the hope of having them reduced. If the syringes were regarded by the court as weapons, and if they were found guilty of threatening injury to a minor, that could mean an extra twenty years in prison. While if they were found guilty on the reduced charge of accessory to kidnapping, they could be out in as little as three years.

The victim impact statements from Kate and Libby would be critical in this.

"One of the scientists, a Dr Furnet, was a blind reviewer on a grant. That means he reviewed it anonymously," the inspector explained.

"He'd reviewed a grant application proposing to explore cases like Kate and Libby's and describing in general terms the Airlie-Kate experiences at camp. He had been very negative about the proposal, claiming that 'real evidence is needed, not second-hand fairy tales'. And yes, one of the people from camp was a named investigator on the grant application, as well as an associated ethics application."

"Wow," interjected Peter. "What's going to happen to them?"

"Dr Furnet has been charged with kidnapping and conspiracy to abduct, and is being investigated by the funding body for violations of the reviewing process. Their lawyer was very concerned by Libby's impact statement and recommended their cooperation to avoid the charge being raised to serious aggregated kidnapping. Our scientist is being prosecuted for violation of the confidentiality agreement he signed, and may also face charges under the Official Secrets Act — which was cited in it. She is also being investigated by the funding organization in relation to the disclosure of confidential information in the grant application."

"How do we protect Airlie and the other gifted students?" asked Airlie's mum. "Even though the kidnapping was kept quiet, a multiple kidnapping trial involving foreign agents is going to get media attention."

"Yes, the cat is somewhat out of the bag."

Sooty meowed from her viewing platform and jumped down to get some attention from the inspector, who scratched his head absentmindedly as he continued. "The court will keep all mention of the victims and the motives in closed session, indeed it maybe that the judge determines that only sentencing will be in open session due to the involvement of minors, not to mention the various national security implications. The funding body will get a special allocation of funds with controlled reviewing for any projects related to the quantum gifts. But the foreign government could very well reveal the details from the grant application. They are already posturing about new discoveries and the right to full disclosure."

"So what are you going to do to protect Airlie and her friends?" Airlie's father growled out. "They can't just go back to school, life as normal."

"And what about me? And Mum and Dad?" Peter asked. "The whole family is at risk."

"Are you showing signs of a talent?" El wondered.

"Not really, just a funny feeling sometimes. But Airlie has never managed to connect to me, and the inspector seems to have more of a connection to Sooty than I do."

"The biggest problem is school," answered the inspector, returning to Mum and Dad's questions. "We've already invited the camp kids and others to the new Opportunity Classes at the Maths and Science School, but will now be making that a formally distinct Maths and Science Middle School that serves the entire state and will take boarders. We will have to take over some nearby college accommodation. And we will take 'funny feelers' in both the Middle School and the High School — particularly siblings and close friends of the gifted kids or the gifted pets. Interestingly, the age at which the gifts show seems to be very specific — and older people seem just to get those funny feelings."

"But I don't want to board," Airlie responded.

"That's something you and your friends and family will have to discuss." The inspector flicked out his hands in a flamboyant gesture that encompassed everyone.

"We are open to ideas, but can't put round-the-clock, year-round, police cars at every student's door. However, boarding fees will be covered by scholarships — at least for the first year — and beyond that for students with notable gifts (quantum and otherwise). But it's going to be a very special school and, as Dean of Students, I'm going to need your help, Airlie! We need to figure out how to make it work. I'd like you to be our first School Captain."

"But there hasn't been an election."

"Actually, there has. Do you remember that survey question asking which student you thought could best represent you? Boys and girls alike, you were the *only* person who put down someone *other* than you."

THE END

Sooty, Airlie and friends will be back in ...

School for PsyQ

For those who purchased a Kindle eBook, this short link should take you to the appropriate review page: http://tiny.cc/AmarevTPQ.

If you can't click links in your eBook reader, then maybe you can scan this QR code:

Reviews, even just ratings, are always appreciated and encourage an author to write more, as well as helping new readers find our books. (If just rating it, and you don't have the time to write a review, you can send your message by upvoting reviews that capture your views.)

You can also reach me at marti24ward@gmail.com. Of course, I can be busy at times, and I also deal with interesting questions in my blog https://martiward.blogspot.com/ — particularly questions about the science and technology (which is all real).